WOLF DESTINIES

ROCKY MOUNTAIN PACK

LUCÍA ASHTA

WOLF
DESTINIES

WOLF DESTINIES

ROCKY MOUNTAIN PACK BOOK FOUR

LUCÍA ASHTA

Wolf Destinies

Rocky Mountain Pack ~ Book Four

Cover design by Sanja Balan of Sanja's Covers

Editing by Ocean's Edge Editing

Proofreading by Geesey Editorial Services

For Nicole,
a wonderful friend.
May we enjoy many more winding hikes together
through enchanted forests.

♥

And also for my daughters and beloved.
Always and forever.

Forge a path through the storm, and the sun will shine again. And if it doesn't, make your own damn rainbows.

NAYA WOLF

WOLF DESTINIES

CHAPTER ONE

NAYA

NAYA SLIPPED OUT from under Bruno's arm, heavy as it draped across her bare torso and the thin pink line that sliced across it. Her injury had been grave enough that not even her wolf healing had managed to put her back together again without a mark. The scar was a constant reminder of how close she'd come to losing everything—and to failing at doing her part to rescue werewolves from the brink of extinction.

Sliding out of bed, she winced when the bed creaked, then tiptoed around the bedroom slash living room to assemble a complete workout outfit. She was in the process of stepping into spandex shorts when heat trailed up her naked body.

She glanced toward the bed. Bruno hadn't moved, save to open his eyes and pin his stare on her.

He groaned and rolled over in bed to fully face her. "Sneaking out again? You need to rest more."

Naya didn't bother to point out that she hadn't managed to "sneak out" even once without Bruno waking up.

"I can't sleep. I'm fidgety all over." Naya pulled a sports crop top over her head and tugged it beneath her breasts.

Bruno groaned another time. "If you're fidgety, that just means you should come back to bed with me, *peligrosa*." He offered her a crooked grin that was so dangerous he perfectly fit the nickname he'd given her.

Naya paused in her dressing, allowing her attention to sweep greedily across his naked and mostly visible form. What wasn't visible beneath a swath of sheet was busy tenting it.

She dragged her teeth across her lower lip. "You don't make the decision easy..."

"I don't mean to."

She stared at him some more, wondering if she was crazy for walking away from their shared bed to go beat the crap out of a punching bag.

"It's been too long without any news of Meiling," she said. Nearly six weeks! "I can't stand it. I've got to do something about it."

He pushed up onto an elbow. "Working out until you're ready to pass out isn't going to help find her."

"I know, but I have to do something, anything."

"You know Maverick, alphas across the world, and even those weird wizards that I've grown to like so much, are all scouring their connections for news of Meiling. We just have to wait."

She flung her hands in the air and paced in her bare feet. "I'm sick of waiting. She needs me!"

"Sí, she probably could use our help. That immortal is no ordinary opponent. But she's no longer at Shèng Shān Monastery, our connections are sure of it, so we have to wait until we figure out where Meiling is before we can help her. We can't just charge out blindly without even knowing where she is."

Naya opened her mouth, but before she could say anything Bruno added, "And we can't go making war on the vampire masters just to find out what they know."

"I know." And Naya really did. Not only had there been no word of Meiling, but they hadn't been able to figure out what the remaining immortals of the notorious Five were up to either. The hunters, who were a continual threat, had been unusually silent, and Naya worried it was more than the fact that Zasha, Quannah, and their Smoky Mountain Pack had recently given them a spanking.

Naya ceased her pacing to sit at the edge of the bed. "I just … I can't abandon her. She must be so scared. I can't just leave her alone with that psychotic bitch with a passion for killing."

He took her hand and squeezed. "I know. If it were you out there again, I'd be out of my mind. I'd do anything and everything I could to find you and get you out of wherever you were. And I like Meiling —a lot. She's your sister, she's Lara's sister, and not only is she important to the two of you, who are very important to me, but the three of you hold in your blood the survival of an entire kind of magical being. If there were something we could do to go help her, *te prometo*, I'd be up and dressed and ready to go in an instant. We'd be on our way right now—tonight."

Naya sighed, squeezing Bruno's hand back.

He added, "You have a responsibility that is greater than any one of you. You must survive. I say that especially for me, because now, *mi corazón*, my heart, it couldn't take losing you. I can't even breathe when I think about something happening to you."

Naya smiled sadly. It couldn't be easy loving her, not when she had a large fluorescent target on her back.

Bruno's eyes were heavy. "You can't risk yourself,

not even to save your sister. The best thing you can do for her is make sure you stay alive."

"The best thing I can do for her, or for were-wolves? Because I'm pretty sure what we want hasn't been important, like, ever."

He sighed and slid across the bed so he could wrap an arm around her waist. "I understand more than most what it feels like for you. Even with Lara, I could see the burden of who she is on her. She was never able to forget it, not even for one stupid day. But, *bueno*, none of us get to choose who we are. I didn't get a choice about loving one of the most dangerous women in the world. As much as I already love you, I wouldn't have chosen a mate who is at constant risk. Who is actually *hunted* a thousand times more than any of the rest of us. My heart would have chosen someone safer."

Naya stiffened. "Well, no one says you have to stick with me, you know. I'm sure there are a whole pack of single women out there just waiting to jump aboard the hottie train." It was a ridiculous state-ment, of course. She knew it.

"Oh, *peligrosa*, you must know I wouldn't trade you for anything." He skimmed his lips across her thigh before pressing light, feathery kisses along her skin, pebbling it. "Not for the entire world and all its riches. Not for a lifetime of stunning sunsets and beautiful views. Not for all the water in the oceans."

More kisses. More tingles racing up and down her thigh.

"I might not have wished for the woman I love to be one of just three women on the planet most at risk of danger. But now that I've had the good fortune of meeting you, now that I've fallen in love with you, now that my wolf has claimed you ... there isn't a single thing I'd want to change about you. Only to keep you safe and at my side for the rest of our lives."

"The rest of our lives, huh?"

He pushed up to kiss her side, then her neck. "Even that doesn't seem like it will be enough to get my fill of you."

"Hmm," she said, mostly because she was losing track of her argument, along with her determination to go anywhere but back into bed with him.

"Forget about our problems for a little while, and allow me to show you all the things you can look forward to for the rest of our lives together."

The rest of their lives was a tall, potentially overwhelming, order. But Sister Wolf would go on strike if Naya so much as entertained a drop of doubt about how suited she and Bruno—and their wolves—were to each other. His wolf had claimed hers, and hers had claimed his. Without hesitation or doubt, their wolves had bonded together. Unburdened by the overthinking tendencies of the rational human mind, they'd acted on instinct and knowing.

Their mate bond was for a lifetime. Naya and Bruno would grow old together over the centuries—assuming they survived Cassia.

"Fine," she said, pretending to be petulant when excitement already zinged through her body like an addictive drug. "I suppose I can spare an hour or so."

"An hour?" He tsked, kissing her jaw so lightly that a shiver jolted her shoulders. "Don't be stingy, *peligrosa*. An hour isn't nearly enough for all the things I have planned for you."

"Oh? Tell me more."

He shook his head, dragging his lips across her cheek. "Showing is so much more fun than telling..."

He pulled her back down to the bed and stripped her out of her clothes in seconds. Two-and-a-half hours later, he'd convinced her that telling had nothing on showing, and that she should revisit her priorities.

But when her limbs felt as wobbly as a gelatin mold, Bruno, who was already proving he knew her perhaps better than she knew herself, jumped out of bed and started dressing, tossing her clothes at her.

"Come on," he said. "Let's spar. Then, when

you're so spent you're incapable of fidgeting, I'll wash you in the shower and tuck you back in bed."

"I'm already incapable of fidgeting."

He grinned. "Good, then maybe I'll finally kick that fine ass of yours in the ring."

The laugh bubbled out of her before she expected it, shooting energy through her languid body. She sat and bounded out of bed. "Not a chance, mister. I know your moves now. I have the upper hand."

He tugged on a t-shirt and kissed her, long and hard enough to suggest he might have been as tempted as she was to tumble back into bed.

"You've had the upper hand since I first laid eyes on you," he whispered. "That still doesn't mean you'll be able to beat me. I'm resourceful."

"Let's see, shall we?" She tugged on the last of her clothes, walked out the door, and winked over her shoulder at him.

He missed the teasing gesture, too busy checking out the rest of her. She laughed into the night, tinged with the suggestion of dawn, and jumped off the porch, running toward the heart of the complex where the training gym was, fully hoping he'd catch her before she arrived.

CHAPTER TWO

NAYA

DESPITE THE PRE-DAWN HOUR, the training gym was packed when Naya and Bruno arrived. Maverick had called in pack shifters from the satellite locations of Idaho, Montana, and Wyoming, and even those into Canada. Their numbers had almost doubled in the past week. All the guest cabins were occupied, and most of the full-time Moonlit Mountains wolves now had roommates, an argument Naya had leaned into whenever her alpha, beta, or gamma narrowed their eyes at her and Bruno as they emerged together from her cabin. They'd get over it soon enough, and they likely wouldn't have had a problem with the arrangement at all if she weren't the lucky savior of werewolves. No one, not even pack leaders, disputed the importance of mate bonds, and it was rarely expected that any of them should wait to form the bond until after an official commit-ment ceremony. But as usual, everything was different when it came to her, and special rules applied.

She was well and bloody sick of the "special" treatment.

The din of shifters smacking pads, bags, and each other, mixed with the low hum of conversation, the occasional shout and grunt of effort, and the buzz of many predators on high alert. Weights clanked, and the muffled shots from the shooting range on the other side of the soundproofed wall, insufficiently muted for preternatural hearing, thumped dully as they hit their targets. Naya could all but reach out and pluck the tension in the air.

Both rings were occupied, as were several of the mats, the climbing treadmill, and much of the general exercise equipment.

Howie and Jeb occupied one of the mats, chasing each other back and forth with sharp blades instead of the wooden swords the pack usually practiced with. A rivulet of blood trailed down Howie's arm, and Jeb was sporting a shallow slash across his stomach.

No one was in the mood to pull their punches...

Someone jumped on Naya's back. Memories of Meiling doing the same to Naya before she'd known she was her sister flashed through Naya's mind as she grabbed her attacker's arm with a steel grip, wrenched her loose of her back, and flung her over her body.

Clove landed on the rubber floor of the gym with a loud thump, her open mouth sucking in air, her eyes wide as if she hadn't expected that.

Had memories not distracted Naya, or perhaps had she been paying closer attention, she would have realized sooner that her attacker was her best friend. She'd realized in mid-flip—too late.

Few could be as light on their feet as Clove, who was short and slender, and spent so much of her time not bothering to touch the ground. Naya should have known—although ... she might have tossed her anyway.

"What the hell, Ni?" Clove eked out when she finally caught her breath. "What kind of welcome is that?"

Naya reached a hand down to her friend, while Bruno watched on, aiming a scowl at Clove. Naya said, "It's the kind of welcome you deserve for sneaking up on me like that."

Clove frowned. "I was just having some fun. You didn't have to beat the shit out of me."

"If she'd beaten the shit out of you, you'd know," Bruno said, rubbing his shoulder where Naya had planted a particularly solid blow the day before. "Trust me."

Clove *pffted*. "Like I need you to tell me my girl's a fucking badass. You've only known her for two months, less even. I've known her my whole life. I *know* how hard she could kick my ass if she wanted to."

"Then what are you whining about?" Bruno asked.

Her mouth dropped open before she recovered. "I am *not* whining. I am *playing*. Does no one around here recognize the fucking difference anymore? Jeeesh. Everyone's on edge all the time lately."

"Yeah, I wonder why," Naya said, but she wrapped an arm around Clove's shoulders and pulled her in for a side hug. "I'm about to jump out of my skin. I can't take much more of this. We gotta find the bitch, pronto."

Naya didn't bother clarifying who the bitch was; Clove had been the one referring to Cassia that way until the moniker stuck.

Clove leaned into Naya. "I hope I get to find her first. I'm gonna pluck her eyeballs out of her head like they're juicy grape tomatoes." She plunked a closed fist into her open palm. "She messed with my sister, she's gonna get a taste of the Clove Stove."

Naya chuckled, pulling Clove closer. "That's an

... inventive one. What, 'cause you blow shit up?" A thing Clove didn't really do, but Naya wouldn't put anything past the petite woman when she was determined.

"No, though I will blow shit up if I have to, you know that. But it's 'cause I got a fire burning inside that can't be put out. I'll go and go and fight and fight till I pluck some tasty grape tomatoes and pop them as an appetizer."

"Ew, that's really gross. Ya coulda just 'killed a bitch' and called it a day."

Clove shook her head and stepped out of Naya's embrace, her dark pixie hair sticking up all over her head, and she still somehow made the crazy haircut look cute, if a bit unhinged. "The bitch is gross, not what I'm gonna do to her. She kills and makes a spectacle of it. Someone like that deserves the grape-tomato treatment. Isn't that right, Bruno?"

"*Sí.* Absolutely."

It was the only time Clove and Bruno agreed on anything. Together, they'd punish Cassia for all she did to Naya until there wasn't much more than a fragment of her left.

Before Clove and Bruno could get going on yet another murderous rant, Naya asked, "So, what's up? How come you're here instead of sleeping or up in the trees?"

"Because shit's gotten real, Ni. *Real*. I'm jumpy as a motherfucker. My mom even tried to dose me with a disgusting valerian root, chamomile, and melatonin concoction she made. Now that was gross."

"Wow," Naya said. "She must be really desperate. She knows you won't drink anything unless it tastes good."

"She says I'm driving her crazy with all my can't-sit-still-ness. But I tell you, she's the one driving *me* crazy."

Naya took a moment to feel badly for Clove's dad, stuck between two fiery women used to doing things their own way.

"So, any news?" Naya asked Clove.

"Nope. We're no closer to getting the bitch."

"And Meiling?"

"Not a word, from what I've heard, but as you know Mav doesn't exactly keep me in the loop."

No, he didn't, especially not now that he was on the periphery of his own pack. Naya was still desperate enough to ask.

"But I did hear the weird mage dudes were asking where you were."

Naya's brows rose. "Albacus and Mordecai?" Though who else could it be?

"Yup."

"So they're back from, well, wherever they went this time?"

"Ah-hah. Just saw them like half an hour ago."

Albacus and Mordecai had been at the pack compound off and on since they'd returned from China. They were like hounds who'd caught a scent, as determined as any of them to understand the mystery of Cassia the immortal, and how to end her. They traveled regularly from the Magical Arts Academy somewhere in France to the Magical Creatures Academy somewhere in the American Southwest, and back again, making other stops they mentioned only in the most vague and secretive of terms, searching everywhere for materials that would reveal how to deliver the kill shot to someone who was supposedly unkillable.

The bookish wizards arrived each time with a stack of ancient-looking books and an excited twinkle in their light eyes. They left again after a few mutters under their breaths that suggested they didn't expect information to be *this* hard to find. But the bastards didn't give up, and Naya had grown quite fond of them over the last several weeks. They were weird as weird got, and she still hadn't gotten used to being able to stare right through them, but she didn't think they could have chosen any better allies to have on their side. Half the time, she barely understood what they were saying, especially during their more feverish discussions back and forth about this ancient spell, or this rare magic, this longshot attempt that might just do it.

A loud pop cracked in the air, leaving Naya's one ear ringing. She went to rub her ear, but ended up smacking something instead...

"Ow," a small, high-pitched voice complained. "Mind what you do with that block of meat there, will ya?"

"Oh my God," Clove said. "It's a little tiny woman."

Said little tiny woman spun in the air, planted her hands on her hips, and narrowed grape-seed-sized eyes on Clove. "Did nobody consider you worthy of the time to teach you manners? Do I *look* like a *woman* to you?"

When a mischievous smile spread across Clove's face, the apparently not-tiny-woman didn't let her speak. Instead, she puffed up her diminutive chest, her proportionately small boobs in a sparkling red crop top, and announced, "I am a fairy. *A fairy.* Make note of it so you don't ever forget and insult another of my kind. I'm Fianna the Crimson."

"Ah," Clove said. "Due to the red hair and red skirt."

"Did I say 'red'?" Fianna the Crimson scowled,

shaking her head in lament. "On top of it all, the poor woman is colorblind."

"Hey," Clove started—

Naya interrupted. "Hi, Fianna the *Crimson*. I'm Naya. Were you looking for ... me? Were you just flying by...?"

It was a ridiculous question, really; it wasn't as if fairies flew around the pack's territory on the regular. Naya had never even seen a fairy before; she'd always thought they were fairytale creatures, as improbable as her finding her mate.

"If you're Naya, I was looking for you," Fianna said.

Bruno was in the process of stepping toward the little fairy when one of the pack wolves called him over. He glanced over his shoulder, then back at the women.

He said, "Fianna the Crimson, I'm Bruno García Vega, beta of the Andes Mountain Pack. It is a pleasure to meet you. I've heard magnificent things about your kind."

A pink blush colored the diminutive fairy's cheeks, and she primped her hair. "Well, now, it's a pleasure to meet *you*, Bruno García Vega, beta of the whatever pack. You look to be worth my time."

Bruno gave her a melt-your-little-tiny-panties smile—Naya didn't think he could help himself, he was just that smoking—that made Fianna giggle like a bell. "If you'll please excuse me," he said, "I'm needed elsewhere at the moment. I'll catch up with you as soon as I can. Naya is my mate."

Then Bruno kissed Naya on the lips until she was practically panting and no one could have any doubts about the validity of his claim, turned, and walked off. Naya tracked his every step until he met up with the pack wolf and left the large athletic facility.

"Woooeyyyy," Fianna said, closely echoing Naya's thoughts. "Some girls have all the luck."

"That's what I'm saying," Clove added. "I wouldn't mind having me some of that."

Naya spun to glare at her best friend.

Clove looked up. "Ooops. Sorry, Ni. I forgot he was yours for a second. A man like that can make a girl forget her own name and birthday."

On that, Clove was right; Bruno could enchant with a single upturn of those full, sensuous lips.

"But really, sorry, Ni," Clove went on. "I forgot myself for real, but it won't happen again, I swear. I know full well that man's as taken as taken gets. But damn, is he ever fine."

"Super fine," Fianna said, wistful and soft like a spring breeze.

Naya pinned a glare on the fairy, who simply

shrugged. "Can't blame a fairy for admiring something beautiful."

"I see that's an easy excuse for both of you."

"I know a fine man when I see one, no matter what the size. But don't worry, I'm not competition. I have my own hot man to keep me entertained, and he's just my size."

"Oooh," Clove said. "Fairy sex. Kinky."

Again, Fianna glowered at Clove, looking down at her from where she hovered at head height, her iridescent, translucent wings a blur from how quickly they were beating; they buzzed softly, like a hummingbird's—a perfect comparison as she was roughly the same size.

"I don't appreciate you making assumptions about what I do with my love life and how far I'm willing to take things, and I certainly don't appreciate you passing judgment on how I decide to have my fun."

Clove put her hands up in surrender. "I'm the last one to judge anyone for getting their rocks off, trust me. You do you, girl. Live it up."

"What does my time with Brodie have to do with rocks? We're both smart enough to leave rocks right where they belong—on the ground, where they don't hurt anybody."

Aware that Clove could lead just about anyone

on a whole itinerary of tangents and detours, Naya stepped between Clove and the fairy. "What do you need me for? I'm happy to help if I can." She tried to stop herself, but couldn't. "I'll even heave rocks out of your way if you need me to."

"Rocks? What?" Fianna's forehead was scrunched into adorable lines so thin they looked like hairs sweeping horizontally across her face.

"What do you want me for?" Naya asked, reeling even herself in.

"The great wizards, Albacus and Mordecai of Irele, patrons and founders of the Magical Arts Academy, Magical Creatures Academy, and all the sister institutions, request the honor of your presence."

Naya bent at the waist in a bow that, again, she couldn't resist. Clove chuckled, but Naya didn't dare glance at her friend for fear she'd laugh at the fairy and her formal ways. She didn't want to offend her. She was just so ... cute.

"Follow me," Fianna said, all business now, and zoomed toward the main entrance to the athletic center as fast as her hummingbird counterpart. Naya and Clove jogged to keep up.

At the doors, Fianna stopped and waited for Naya to press it open, calling as she zipped out, "Just Naya, not the other one."

"Where Naya goes, I go," Clove said. "So don't even dream of shaking me."

One side of Fianna's crimson-red mouth arched in mischief, before the fairy flew away so fast that Naya had to sprint to keep up.

Fifty meters down a sidewalk, an alarm rang out across the entire pack compound.

Naya slid to a stop as wolves ran out of buildings all around them, waiting to find out what the siren signified.

Her muscles jumped, wanting to tear off to tackle the threat to her pack.

A howl went up to the west, setting off a chorus of them as the sun cracked the horizon.

Whatever the wizard brothers wanted from her, it'd have to wait.

Clove clutched Naya's hand so she couldn't run off without her. This threat, Clove said silently, they'd face together.

CHAPTER THREE

NAYA

IN LESS THAN A MINUTE, a circle of shifters, both in human and wolf forms, circled Naya, and Clove by extension, who continued to grip Naya's hand as if it were the only way to guarantee Naya wouldn't again disappear from right within the supposed safety of pack territory. What Clove would do to keep her safe against an immortal who could literally fly, Naya couldn't guess at, but she had no doubt her friend would give it everything she had. Clove was fierce enough to make up for her petite size.

Within five minutes, the circle had expanded to encompass several rows of growling, murderous shifters. Some of those in human form held weapons: swords, knives, silver-loaded guns. Howie held nunchucks and Jeb double-fisted shiny and wickedly-sharp katanas.

Bruno had pushed his way past the concentric circles of shifters to stand beside her, where he only glanced at her occasionally, focused on scenting, listening, and scanning the lightening sky for any sign of the source of the alarm.

Maverick bounded toward them in his wolf form, River and Blake directly behind him. Their three wolves were the largest and strongest in the entire pack. In mid-leap, Maverick shifted into a man, unconcerned by his sudden nudity as he studied their surroundings for several moments in silence, no doubt attempting to determine whether they were safe where they stood. It was the first time Naya had been in such close proximity to him in weeks. Evidently, he considered whatever threat they now faced more important than the constant possibility that Cassia might read his thoughts.

Mordecai and Albacus floated over moments later, and Fianna, who still hovered beside Naya, was the first to slice through the tangible tension that thickened the otherwise crisp mountain air.

"Somebody had better tell me what's going on soon." Fianna flashed her open palms, the sparkling magic sparking from her hands a bright red that matched the rest of her. "I need to know where to point these." She wiggled her fingers and curled her lip in a vicious snarl.

Though the fairy was smaller than any one of their paws, not a single Rocky Mountain Pack wolf scoffed. In fact, Maverick tipped his head at her. In the world of magic, size didn't always matter, and allies were appreciated no matter what shape they came in.

In a strong voice that carried the power of his alpha wolf, Maverick said, "Our scouts have caught sight of the immortal ... Cassia."

Growls, snarls, and gasps of surprise circled their group, before lapsing into a stunned yet explosive quiet.

Fighting was imminent. One of Naya's triceps twitched in anticipation, visibly jumping.

Maverick continued: "Just in time, the mages figured out how to protect me from her mental interference." Though he spoke aloud, Naya heard his announcement echoed within her mind. He was also broadcasting telepathically for the rest of the pack. "Took them fucking long enough, *shit*," he added just for his wolves. Then again for everyone: "We don't know what she's here for yet"—several stares pointed at Naya—"but we have to assume she's trying to get at Naya again."

The responding growls and snarls were so vicious

that a shiver raced up Naya's spine. Every Rocky Mountain Pack wolf would defend her to the death, as would Bruno.

But Cassia was an immortal. Despite their continued efforts, the mages hadn't yet discovered how to end the woman whom, by definition, couldn't be killed.

Her stomach churned, and sudden nerves made her jumpy. How many of her friends and loved ones would survive the onslaught Cassia no doubt intended?

She couldn't sacrifice herself to save her pack; she had to save all the werewolves in her pack and beyond. That was her responsibility, the one she couldn't escape.

But what if Cassia got to her in the end anyway? No matter how hard she fought, or how bravely her pack protected her? Everyone she loved might die. What if she lost her mate when she'd only just found him? She couldn't be the cause of the destruction of her pack, she just *couldn't*.

"I can scent your fear," Maverick said, and it wasn't a reprimand for the wolves who'd trained relentlessly to defend against the usual enemies of wolf shifters.

There was nothing ordinary about Cassia.

"But we won't let the immortal get to Naya. She

was spotted at the far boundary of pack land, so even if the fucker starts flying, we've still got a little time." His eyes grew stormy, his mouth a pissed-off line. "When she gets here, we *will* fight. We'll defend Naya at all costs. We'll throw everything we've got at the bitch until something sticks."

Bile rose up Naya's throat; she had to forcefully swallow it down. "If you fight to protect me, you'll die."

She hadn't meant to say that, she hadn't meant to speak at all, but once the words were out, she wouldn't take them back.

She wouldn't let anyone else die for a lost cause.

"Unless Albacus and Mordecai have discovered a way to kill Cassia that I don't know about, you'll all just die trying to protect me, and in the end, even if we blow her to smithereens, she'll just piece herself back together and come back to life, and *then* come get me. We all heard Zasha and Quannah of the Smoky Mountain Pack. The bloody bastards can't be killed. Even when it looks like they can't possibly survive, they do."

"No, Naya," Maverick said, and as her alpha, Naya's duty was to obey.

Screw duty. Duty was what had gotten her into this mess in the first place.

"I won't be responsible for all of you dying over me."

"You don't get to decide what the wolves of this pack do," Maverick said, his eyes flashing the gold of their pack's magic. "I'm the alpha, a fact which you seem to have forgotten."

"I haven't forgotten for a second, and with all due respect, how could I live with myself if you all die for me? How could I go on after that?"

"Your only job is to survive, no matter what," Maverick said. "That's all you need to worry about."

Naya tsked. "Yeah, right. Because why would I care that every single person I know might die today over some stupid asshole who just takes whatever she wants?"

The growls from the wolves surrounding her were continuous now, though Naya couldn't decide whether they were angry at Cassia, her, or both, or perhaps simply the circumstances, which had pitted wolves against the world from the very beginning. There wasn't a single wolf shifter alive who wasn't hunted simply for their nature.

"You know how this works as well as I do. None of us choose our roles within a pack. The magic does that. Just as I was chosen as alpha because I'm capable of leading through challenges such as these, you were chosen to ensure werewolves survive centuries from now." He paused, looking out at his pack. "Cassia won't come anywhere near you, Ni," Maverick said, his voice a determined rumble. "She won't touch you."

A few of the wolves called out some encouraging *yeahs*, *that's rights*, and *fuck yeahs*, and while Naya appreciated the sentiment, none of them had witnessed Cassia in action at Shèng Shān Monastery as she had. Not only was the woman practically all-powerful, she was cruel and vicious. She'd made that vampire master suffer needlessly before she killed him, and she'd made a spectacle of it. A dark creature like that wouldn't stop until she was made to.

"Mav," Naya started, knowing full well she was pushing the limits of the alpha-pack wolf role, as well as of the putative-father-daughter dynamic. "May I ask, have Albacus or Mordecai discovered a way to kill her?"

As one, the attention of the wolves around her slid to the translucent wizards.

Maverick, however, glared at her, before calling over his shoulder to them, "Go ahead. Tell them."

"Well," Mordecai started, jingling the runes in his pocket, their melodic tinkling at odds with the aggressive atmosphere of their gathering. "We've been studying every book on the matter that we can think of."

"Every one we can get our hands on," Albacus said. "And that's quite a lot. We've amassed extensive libraries all over the world."

"At every one of our castles and campuses."

"We inherited our ancestors' vast libraries as well, and we've been collecting new books on magic—"

"Rare magic, dark magic, ancient magic," Mordecai interjected. "Everything we've been able to find to ensure we have the most complete source of information on the magical world and communities as is possible."

"We've even taken loans from the Magical Council's library, all in search of information on immortals such as Cassia."

"And?" Blake asked, when the pack gamma should have remained quiet, waiting for their alpha to lead the direction of this discussion. But Naya understood why even someone as aware of his role as Blake would speak up. The wizards believed in detours, wandering leisurely strolls, and the long way around absolutely every topic, and Cassia was a few hundred acres away, when not even a few hundred countries was enough distance.

Naya liked the wizards very much, but that didn't change the fact that they made her twitch all over with impatience. Blake pressed his lips shut in a grim line and dipped his head in unspoken apology at Maverick.

"We found..." Mordecai jiggled the pockets of his robes, eliciting more tinkling. "Well, we found little."

Albacus shook his head in lament, setting off a second harmony as the beads capping the many braids in his hair clanked together softly. "With how hard and how far we looked, we should have found quite a lot of information. We read many languages and even scoured ancient texts that no one believes to exist anymore. Those are our favorites..."

"All we found were whispers."

"Hints."

"As if even the writers of these tomes were afraid to mention the immortals."

"We had to read between the lines," Albacus said, "to gather any information at all."

They all waited on bated breath.

"Well?" Maverick snapped with another flash of gold eyes. Several of the other shifters in wolf form transformed into their human shapes as if to better absorb whatever the wizards were about to say next. "Don't keep us hanging any longer," Maverick said. "You're literally torturing us here while we've got a homicidal maniac on the way. Is there anything we can do to take her out?"

Even Fianna, who'd sung the mages' full titles in

adulation looked ready to pop as her little crimson mouth waggled back and forth and magic sparked from her hands, seemingly without meaning to.

"From what we've been able to deduce..." Albacus said.

"There are two possible ways for an individual to become an immortal," Mordecai added.

"We don't think that immortality as what Cassia possesses can be passed on through the reproductive process, as with wolf shifters."

"Or with many other types of shifters either."

"Right," Albacus said. "From what we could gather, the immortality she has was either gifted to her through a spell—"

"Though it's perhaps more of a curse than a gift, depending on outlook."

Albacus nodded to another tinkle of chimes. "That depends on the individual, of course, and their personal disposition toward eternal life." He paused, and as one, they all seemed to lean toward the wizened wizard as the sun rose, visible through his half-opaque body.

Bruno wrapped an arm around Naya's waist, pulling her closer.

Albacus' voice crackled for a moment as he added, "Either Cassia received her gift—or curse," he glanced at his brother, "through a spell ... or she received it through some sort of energy transference borne in a mage's specific and unique adaptation of magic. We presume that she was unable to do this herself since she doesn't appear to have the full range of magic or learnedness of a trained witch or wizard."

"Though it's not an option we can rule out entirely and remain thorough," Mordecai added.

Say what?

"Break it down for us," Maverick said. "And quickly. Please."

Albacus' and Mordecai's faces scrunched in similar expressions of confusion.

"Why...?" Albacus began.

"Why would we break our theory when we only just finished putting it together?" Mordecai completed.

Fianna cleared her throat. "It'd probably help if you all kept in mind that the Lords Mordecai and Albacus have lived for many centuries. Idioms and expressions change faster than they do. They aren't as quick to adapt to the times as I am." She pushed out her chest in what appeared to be pride.

"Just ... explain," Maverick said, gruff but trying to remain patient. If he felt anything like Naya, he might explode before the brothers got around to spitting out anything intelligible.

Mordecai's eyes unfocused as he stared out into

space, perhaps lost in thought, but he was the one to say, "Either Cassia received her immortality via a spell, which would be the best-case scenario, or through a blast of intuitive magic from an unknown sorcerer."

Albacus said, "It's also possible that there is a third option that we're wholly unaware of."

"Though it's unlikely."

"Very," Fianna added in a sweet voice. "If you two don't know about it, I highly doubt anyone does. Even if it happened over a thousand years ago."

"It's true," Mordecai and Albacus said together for once.

"We are experts in our fields," Mordecai added, and Albacus nodded to another round of beads tinkling.

"And as foremost experts in magic," Mordecai said, "if Cassia received her immortality through a spell, and we can manage to piece that spell together, we have a chance at undoing the spell entirely. A very fine chance indeed."

"But we'll need to figure out the original spell as close to exactly as possible, or else it'd be dangerous to mess with it at all."

"Not just for her, but potentially for all of us."

"Around the globe." Albacus gave a somber nod.

"A spell powerful enough to grant eternal life might have perilous repercussions if messed with."

"And that's assuming there aren't failsafes built into the spell."

"To prevent just this type of meddling, you see," Albacus said.

"Okay," Mav said. "How close are you to piecing the original spell together?"

"At the very beginning," Albacus said. "We haven't been able to verify that it's a spell at all at this point—not that it really matters."

"And why wouldn't it matter?" Maverick asked. "You just said it matters a whole hell of a lot."

"It won't matter," Mordecai said, "because if it's not a spell, and it *is* what my brother and I enjoy calling *intuitive* magic, then there's no way we can deduce enough of the original magic to counteract it. Intuitive magic is too unique to the wielder."

"The magic has, how shall I say it...?" Albacus ran a knobby hand along the length of his long beard for a few moments. "Think of it as if the magic has personality. My brother and I would have to know if the mage who designed the immortality magic were quick to anger or slow to enrage, impulsive or measured, quiet or loud, intelligent or dimwitted—"

"Well, the magician would definitely not be dimwitted," Mordecai said, "they'd be quite bright, that bit we can already know. No one lesser could create eternal life from one that was finite."

Albacus scowled. "It was nothing more than an illustrative example, of course."

Mordecai waved at his brother dismissively while tilting his head in consideration. "However, we wouldn't necessarily be able to tell whether the mage believed he or she was practicing dark or light magic."

"True, brother, true. It's possible the mage believed what they were doing was good." Albacus shrugged. "Even the brightest minds can be deceived and make mistakes."

"I'll be sure to remember that," Mav said with a frown. "So what's the next step in figuring out what to do about the immortality magic?" And while Maverick waited for a response, he pointed meaningful looks at several of his wolves, who tore off at a full-out run. No doubt, he was directing them to take steps to prepare for Cassia's arrival via the pack's telepathic link.

"We study the immortal," Albacus said with far too much pep.

"Um," Naya said, then pinched her mouth shut at a look from Maverick.

"Well?" he finally snapped at her. "You may as well tell us. The immortal's here already. It's now or never, and time's ticking." The depth of his scowl added, *I should've never told the wizards we had time to spare.*

"I spent more time than I'd like with Cassia, right?" Naya said while Bruno's hand clamped on her hip as if he could barely stand the reminder. She smiled at him reassuringly, though she herself felt far from reassured. "Uh," Naya hedged. "Well..." Then she spit it out in one big rush. "Cassia's a coldhearted killer. She'll murder the both of you. Even if you are half, ah, dead?"

"We like to think we're half alive," Albacus said with a soft smile that peeked through bushy beard and mustache. "We're optimists, my brother and I. We do love living."

Mordecai smiled too. "Or half living, as it were."

"Right," Naya said, swallowing a silent, *Then you'd better hurry the fuck up before Maverick blows a gasket and figures out how to strangle you both.* "Even if you're half alive, Cassia will find the way to kill you for good. She's murderous and mean and vicious and ... and she can freaking *fly*, okay? *She can fly.* Even these grandmaster pooh-bah vampires were afraid of her, and trust me, they were scary as shit."

At that, Albacus' smile dropped, and Mordecai began jingling his runes again. Even the sweet sound of them seemed to grate on her nerves and increase the general level of tension.

She breathed. "She blew up a vampire master. Not just any old vampire, a freaking master bloodsucker. And that's not just a saying. After emptying his body of all life, he went splat. Not an exaggeration. First, he shriveled up like he was a deflating balloon, and then *bam*, blood and guts raining everywhere, and I do mean everywhere. They're never gonna get that room clean."

Despite the frightening imagery, Albacus' eyes were glittering, and Mordecai had frozen mid-jingle.

"She sucked the life out of someone?" Mordecai asked dreamily.

Naya nodded. "Yeah. It was like she kissed him, but instead he just ... shriveled up. It was disgusting."

"The Kiss of Death," Albacus uttered far too reverently. "Gotta admire someone who excels at what they do, even if it is dark and horrendous."

"If you say so," Naya muttered. "I'd rather turn that nasty party trick on her and be done with the woman."

"The *bitch*," Clove growled behind her. "She needs to die already."

At that, several of the shifters surrounding them yipped and offered truncated howls.

"It might help if we could study the girl Naya too," Mordecai said.

Bruno, Mav, River, Blake, and several others snarled at the wizard, and Clove said, "She's no girl," which Naya appreciated.

"Pardon me," Mordecai said. "We're over four-hundred years old. Just about anyone is a child to us."

"Except for Cassia," Albacus said.

"Except for her."

They still sounded far too admiring of the skills of a murderous super villain with an unfair leg up on pretty much everyone else in existence. Even that other immortal, Cyrus, had a healthy respect for her.

"You can't study Naya," Mav said while also silently commanding another few shifters, who ran off to do his bidding.

"No way," Bruno added.

"What if Cassia is somehow connected to Naya and her sisters?" Albacus said. "She seems to show an inordinate amount of interest in them. Perhaps she's linked their magic somehow. And we *must* rid the world of the threat the immortal poses. She's too dangerous. Too unchecked by others or her own moral guidance."

At least they had that fact straight...

"I don't feel connected to her at all, unless you count wanting to kill her," Naya said, really, *really* hoping Cassia hadn't found a way to connect her nastiness to her.

Mordecai shrugged nonchalantly. "No stone unturned, isn't that the saying?"

"Well, this particular stone's gonna remain right where it is," Mav said. "Under my protection and supervision."

She went from being a *girl* to a *stone*. That didn't seem like an upgrade...

"If it might help though..." Naya said as Howie returned with a machine gun leaning against one shoulder, a rocket launcher against the other. Jeb jogged behind him with heavy tote bags in either hand, no doubt filled with more of the same.

"No," Mav and Bruno said right away. For once, the two men were a united front.

"Not a chance," Maverick added.

"*Ni una,*" Bruno echoed. *Not even one.*

"But what if the wizards could discover something helpful through checking me out?" Naya asked. "Something that could keep all of us, all of you, alive?"

"That doesn't sound like the case," Mav said. "It's just a theory, out of a whole bunch of theories they have no way to be certain of. Or am I wrong?"

"No," Mordecai said. "But if we study the immortal, we'll learn more."

"For certain we will," Albacus said. "She can only hide so much from us. One way or another, we'll unearth her secrets. Some, at least. We just have to find the way to contain her safely."

"We're more determined than most," Mordecai added.

"And we have longer than most to figure things out, too," Albacus said.

They might, but Naya didn't. And Meiling sure as shit didn't.

Naya kept trying to reach out and connect to her sister, but she couldn't feel her at all. She didn't even know if she was still alive, or if she'd died scared and alone, all because she'd left the monastery and traveled around the world to warn her.

Naya took half a step forward so she was closer to Mav, though there were still several lines of protectors between them.

"I'm not saying put me in the same room with Cassia—"

Practically every single shifter there snarled in response to her offhand comment, and she committed to speaking more carefully. *Jeez!*

She cleared her throat and refrained from rolling her eyes. "All I'm saying is, what would it hurt for Mordecai and Albacus to examine me? See if they can figure out something about my magic?

We need to do everything we can to defeat Cassia, don't we?"

"We do," Mav said. "But not that."

Why not? she wanted to ask, but she didn't. Maverick was still the alpha, and she'd already overstepped her place within the pack's clearly delineated hierarchy.

The only reason Naya could think of for Mav's refusal was that he didn't trust the mages. Or, more likely, he trusted them in a general manner, he just didn't fully trust them with her specifically when they could affect her magic without any of them realizing it. When it came to her, all the standards were different.

She opened her mouth to protest, shut it, opened it again, but then closed it when Clove of all people squeezed her hand in warning. Mav was already on edge, and nothing Naya said would change his mind. She sighed softly, tamping down her frustration.

How the hell were they supposed to keep Cassia away when she was already on pack land? They had no real plan about how to take her out! All they had was a bunch of *maybes* from weird wizards, and an entire pack about to snap at the barest provocation.

Sister Wolf paced and snarled savagely inside her, ready to rip Cassia apart limb from limb. For all the good it'd do...

The pack was a powder keg, and the match was scraping along a rock, on its way to being lit.

Even Albacus tugged on his beard in annoyance, at their collective helplessness, she assumed. "We'll keep studying the books," he said, more gruffly than she'd ever heard him. "We'll piece together the likeliest elements of the spell used."

"If a spell was used," Mordecai interjected.

"Right, *if*. But if one was used, we should be able to arrange the necessary elements."

"It's impossible to guess at the exact wording," Mordecai said, "which is theoretically quite important. But we've been at this long enough that we should get close enough to be able to work out some sort of counterspell. The nearer we get to the original creation, the more likely it will work."

Albacus was frozen with his mouth hanging open, his forehead scrunched into an accordion of wrinkles. "A simple eavesdropping spell," he whispered in awe.

"A what?" River muttered, but the brothers ignored all of them as they faced each other.

Mordecai was jingling the runes in his pockets repeatedly as his own excitement built. "Genius, brother! It was so simple that we missed it."

"The obvious right in front of our faces. So close we couldn't see the forest for the trees."

"If we can figure out who crafted the spell," Mordecai said.

"We can perhaps spy on them until we find the specific instance in time when Cassia came into their lives!"

"It could take time to find the mage first, and then the instance in their life second..."

"But we could do it," Albacus said, literally jumping up and down in the air, and since he didn't stand on the earth, he floated and bobbed somewhat mesmerizingly.

Fianna clenched her fists, closed her eyes tightly, and squealed. "You did it!"

Seemed a tad early to celebrate, didn't it? They still had an immortal *on their pack property*. Right then. In that precise moment. And she could bend the fucking *air* to her will.

"There aren't too many magicians throughout history powerful enough to do a spell of this magnitude," Albacus said. "Especially a thousand years back, when there were fewer mages in the world."

"And there were also less records kept then, brother, remember that."

"Oh, don't worry." Albacus waved a hand between them. "We'll find a reference. Everyone is eventually a victim of their own hubris. They'll have told someone something."

"And they'll have asked them to keep it a secret," Mordecai said. "But..." He grinned. "Secrets are the first to be shared, aren't they, brother?"

"Always."

Seemed to Naya that the brothers were extrapolating conclusions that didn't necessarily line up, but their faces were mirror images of excitement. Who was she to burst their bubbles, especially when they might actually pull it off?

"Then do it," Mav said. "Just leave Naya out of it. But right now we need your help to contain Cassia before she reaches us. You said you can interfere with the immortal's access to the air element?"

"*Oui*," Albacus said. "We've adapted a spell to fit her. Because she's immortal and we don't yet fully understand the science behind her magic, the spell won't completely disconnect her from the element—"

"It will, however, mute her abilities," Mordecai added. "There'll be no repeat of the fight in the basin of Shèng Shān Mountain. She'll still be able to control the air—"

"But no more than us." Albacus smiled placidly, as if Cassia having *less* control were sufficient to take down the bitch who'd stolen Meiling from right under their translucent noses.

Mav. A voice filtered into Naya's mind, and it wasn't Maverick's or River's. She thought it might be

Cleo's, but she couldn't be sure. Either way, none of the pack wolves would use the link that broadcast to the entire pack unless it was an emergency. Naya squeezed Clove's hand and leaned into Bruno, wondering if these might be the last calm moments they'd share before immortal shit hit the fan.

Though the voice broadcast inside their minds, several of the wolves perked their heads to the side, listening.

We're at the edge of pack land with the immortal, and she keeps saying she isn't Cassia and that she needs to see Naya.

She can make all the claims she wants, Mav answered, *she's not getting anywhere near Naya.*

Yeah, that's what I said, maybe-Cleo continued. *But now she's saying she's actually Meiling, that she did some kind of body swap deal with the bitch, and that she can help us find the real Cassia.*

A pause, during which the alpha perched his hands to either side of his hips, drawing Naya's gaze to his nakedness and what hung just below said hips before she quickly looked away.

Then, *Mav, of course this might be some fucking trick, but ... I believe her. So does Scooby.*

Maverick scowled and narrowed his eyes at an invisible opponent so viciously that Naya flinched.

Fine. I'm coming to see her. But she stays where

she is. She's not getting close to Naya no matter who she claims to be. You've got her contained?

For now, yeah. She's not fighting us. The air's still. She's not doing any magic at all that we can tell.

Maverick glared at no one in particular, his eyes flashing gold for a fast second. "Blake, Mordecai and Albacus, you're with me. River and the rest of you, you stay here. No one gets close to Naya. No one. Understood?"

Yips, snarls, and *yeahs*.

"I should come too," Fianna said. "You never know when my fairy abilities might come in handy."

Given that Naya didn't think a single one of them knew what a fairy who spanned all of two, perhaps three inches, was capable of, Mav nodded once. "Okay. You come too."

He turned and pinned Naya in a stare so ferocious she hadn't seen the likes of it in years. He pointed at her. "Ni, you stay put. I don't care what you hear, see, smell, or feel. You don't move a hair, you got me? You got an itch on your ass, you wait till I get back to scratch it. And you know I mean it."

"Yeah, got it." Naya didn't even bother to keep the resentment from her tone. She fully understood he was just trying to keep her, and by extension all werewolfkind, safe, but did he have to be such an overprotective prick about it? Apparently yes, yes he did. It was the way of alphas, she knew it. Still...

"And you." Mav slid his finger until it pointed at Bruno. "You protect her with your life. Today, you're a Rocky Mountain Pack wolf, you hear me?"

"Loud and clear."

"I'll protect her with my life too," Clove said, finally withdrawing her hand from Naya's to throw some air punches.

"Good," Mav said, then spun to stare at all his wolves once more before returning to Naya. "You stay safe. Promise me."

"I promise." This time, Naya didn't have to temper her reaction. His concern for her was a tangible force that vibrated between them. He loved her.

"I promise, Mav. No risks. I'll stay right here with everyone else."

"Good," he said, and this time his voice was soft, as if he were thinking of just how much they all had to lose.

"I remember why I need to stay alive. It's my duty," she added.

Mav nodded. "Today, you forget about everyone else, and you stay alive for you."

Then he ran off, shifting in mid-stride, Blake doing the same. The wizards zoomed behind the running wolves, as did Fianna, who mumbled under her breath, "Wow. What a day, what a show. So much to see..."

Naya almost chuckled at the fairy's admiration of the fine naked wolf shifters all around them, but was unable to do much beyond think about Meiling and hope her sister was safe.

Somehow.

Despite the cruel, merciless immortal who'd snatched her away.

Despite all odds...

CHAPTER FOUR

NAYA

THE ALARM that alerted the Rocky Mountain Pack of danger had ceased its cautionary blaring as soon as Maverick, Blake, and the others had raced off to confront Cassia. At first, Naya and all the shifters that circled her in a protective formation waited for news from their alpha patiently. But when an entire hour passed, and then a second, and still nothing, even River looked like he might be considering ignoring Mav's orders to go find out what the hell was going on. Or maybe that was just Naya reading into the uncommonly deep scowl that adorned River's otherwise handsome face. Dark scruff and even darker brows, drawn low, shadowed his eyes, making him appear as ferocious as Naya knew the man to be. After himself, he was the one Mav most trusted with the safety of the pack. River was actually probably daydreaming about how he'd dismantle the asshole of an immortal piece by piece, Naya decided. That's why he was directing a death stare off into empty space.

Naya's limited patience wasn't helped by Clove either, who was as fidgety as a five-year-old told to sit still and then given nothing to distract herself with. She was pacing back and forth across the open inner circle, where only she, Naya, and Bruno stood, and which only spanned perhaps ten feet before she bumped the toes of the first line of guards. Every time Clove reached the circle of shifters, at least one of them snarled or hurled some creative cursing at her. The guards were at the point of inventing profanities, most of which involved vivid descriptions of Clove's body parts and where they'd like to shove them, just to get her to stop. She didn't. Clove snapped back with equal ferocity, paced in the opposite direction, then repeated the process with a new set of shifters all over again.

Even Bruno, who refused to move more than a foot away from Naya, tensed every time Clove swept past too closely, which she did often—possibly on purpose. Before long, someone was going to take Clove down and there'd be a brawl. A big one. Even Clove would probably enjoy the diversion.

Any distraction from the mind-numbing anticipation was welcome at this point.

Naya was slowly losing her ever-loving mind—plus, she had to pee. Badly. She hadn't planned to stand in place for hours when she'd first exited the training gym, which felt like a small eternity ago.

But Maverick had told her not to move. It was as direct an order as it got. And her alpha was already on edge. With Cassia on the property, if she disobeyed Maverick now, he was going to lose his shit.

As much as she itched with the desire to tear off into the forest to burn off this frenetic energy and taste the freedom of the vast outdoors, she wouldn't be the cause of that kind of stress in a man she cared for, whom she owed her loyalty to besides.

Pack hierarchy was what it was. Naya wasn't usually a fan of being told what to do, especially as she was on the receiving end of far more directives than any other wolf in their pack. But magic had been appointing the leaders of packs since the beginning of shifters. Now was not the time to argue about its validity—or give Mav an aneurysm.

"Bruno," River called, his voice a tight steel band. "Mav wants you."

Obviously, Mav had been speaking to River through the pack link. River was the only other pack wolf able to single out a person and direct his words only to them.

"What?" Naya protested. "Just him? What about me?"

River gave her a *come on* look, not bothering to hold back on the sarcastic bend to his lips, then added a *What do you think?* tilt of his head for good measure. The sunlight reflected off his dark glossy hair, and Naya wanted to flick him right in the crown, where it was brightest. Of course, none of this was River's fault; none of it was even Maverick's. Didn't do a thing to temper her impulses. She folded her hands in front of her body to keep herself from doing something she might regret later.

"Come on, Riv," Naya said, annoyed to pick up on a whiny edge to her plea. "I'll know if it's really Cassia or if it's Meiling. More than anybody. I've spent more time alone with both of them than anyone else."

"I wouldn't be reminding me of that right now if I were you."

Naya scowled at River; he smiled wickedly, seeming to delight in her spunk. It only made the fire inside Naya flare. And though she was certain he saw it simmering inside her, he finally sighed, running a large hand through his short-cut hair, rubbing forcefully at it.

"Ni, the fucking immortal that we don't know how to kill, but who definitely wants to kill you, is on pack territory. Here. Right now. Give me a fucking break, okay? Stop busting my balls and Mav's, and just be glad he hasn't tried to lock you up somewhere the fucking cunt will never find you."

Bruno growled, a slow and menacing warning that caused the fine hairs on the back of her neck to stand.

River cast a look at him but didn't address him. Instead, he told Naya, "You know as well as I do that Mav's wolf wants to rip the bitch to shreds and then piss on her body for coming after you like she did. But he can't. None of us can. So just sit tight, okay? And for the love of my fucking sanity, Clove, will you stop with your pacing already? I'm having to work double time over here not to let someone pin you down and keep you there until we're sure your legs are ready to stop fucking moving already."

He rubbed both hands across the short, partially spiky strands of hair another time, before grunting.

"Bruno, go."

"Not after that." Bruno closed the space between Naya and him, placing a protective hand at the small of her back.

"Dude, do you actually think I'm gonna hurt her or something? Did you fucking miss the point how we'll all literally die before letting anything happen to her?"

Bruno snarled, "I don't like how you're talking to her."

"Tough shit. I gave you an order, now follow it."

"I'm beta of my own pack, you know. And my wolf is stronger than yours."

If the air had been tense before, it was doubly so now. Wolves around them pretended not to look, but studied their beta for his response regardless.

River clenched and unclenched his jaw, but when he spoke, it was with a forced calm. "Look, man, we're all on edge right now. Naya's in direct danger. Every single one of us wants to fight over who gets to kill this immortal, and joke's on us, none of us can. Today, you're part of the Rocky Mountain Pack. You heard Mav. And in case you didn't realize it, that's an honor. He asked for you to go, so you go." River paused, and added, more softly, as if finally he were talking to a buddy instead of issuing commands: "Dude, for real. Naya's as safe here with us as she is with you. Go."

Bruno stared at River for so long that Naya wasn't sure if he'd do as he was asked. Eventually, however, he squeezed Naya's waist and disengaged from her. He stepped between wolves to emerge from the rows of guards, saying before he left, "I'm honored to be welcomed into this pack, even for a day."

And then, with a single backward look at Naya, where his eyes blazed with heat, with need, and with a fierce determination to keep her safe, he broke into a jog.

"They're at the guardhouse by the main entrance," River called out.

And then Bruno was gone.

Bruno

Peligrosa, *are you okay?* Bruno asked Naya through their mate link. Now that they'd consummated their bond, they could speak to each other telepathically. It was the way for all wolf mates.

He'd only left her side perhaps fifteen minutes ago, and already Brother Wolf was antsy.

Bruno had been a package of tension since learning that Cassia, his beloved's greatest enemy, was close enough to reach her. But only the distance between him and Naya made him feel powerless, like something might happen to her in his absence and he'd never be able to forgive himself. He and Naya had only just begun to connect, and already he worried that he wouldn't be able to live on without her. Sure, he would survive, but his body would be little more than a shell housing broken bits and pieces inside.

As he ran toward the guardhouse that stood like a silent sentinel at the main entrance to the pack complex, twice he nearly turned around to head back to her, and once he actually did, running for several minutes before getting hold of his emotions long enough to convince himself that the best way to help Naya was to make sure Cassia was who she said she was, and if she wasn't actually Meiling—somehow— then to do everything he could to keep the immortal away from his woman. His mate. His everything.

Naya's response took mere seconds to arrive, but even that half a minute was enough to make him spin back around and sprint in her direction.

I'm fine, she assured him, dancing through his mind, and he spun back around again, running the last hundred meters to reach the guardhouse.

I might end up killing my best friend before this is all over, but ya know, fine.

He chuckled. *You could have picked a sweet, docile friend who's happy to just sit around quietly, doing everyone's bidding.*

Naya's laughter filled his mind, reaching even its darkest corners, where the fear of losing her had already made a home. He smiled, drawing to a stop at the stairs leading up to the viewing stand.

Pick Clove? Nah, I never would've picked someone as obnoxious as her. She just grew on me, like a fungus. Like athlete's foot. But I do love the fuck out of her.

Again, she laughed, and the sun seemed to shine more brightly. *I still might have to kill her before the day is over though.*

Fully understood, peligrosa. No one would blame you.

He felt her shift, turning serious. *I need to know what's going on over there. Tell me everything.*

I'm here now. I'll update you when I can. But you keep safe while I'm gone.

Silence.

You hear me, mi amor? You need to stay safe for me.

Don't worry. I have plenty to live for. I haven't gotten even close to getting my fill of you.

Good. Because I'm already thinking of what I want to do with you as soon as we're alone again. Maybe sooner. I'm tired of waiting.

Me and you both. Me and you both. Just ... hurry. And stay safe. Cassia is one cruel fucker. A spike of fear surged across their link. *For real, watch your back. She might say she's Meiling, but how would that even happen? It's probably a trick, and the woman doesn't care who she hurts. In fact ... oh no. She'll want to hurt you to get to me. You should come back.*

I'll be fine. Mav called me here. I have to go up.

Be careful.

Bruno hadn't known Naya a long time, but he already knew her better than he did anyone else. She wasn't prone to fits of panic; she definitely wasn't one to succumb to fear. She was brave, fierce, and determined, all attributes he loved. She could kick even his ass half the time in the ring.

It was the mate connection between them that made them vulnerable, something he hadn't anticipated. It was already so strong, so magical, and so beautiful—so wholly miraculous and fulfilling—that he couldn't imagine being without it.

She'd likely be experiencing some of the same. What they shared was so new that he wanted—needed—the chance to explore it fully. He needed a lifetime filled with her. With all of her.

Remember, I'm as strong as your alpha, he told her in an attempt to soothe the spike of fear still traveling from her to him across their link. *I'll take care of myself. I promise I'll be coming back to you.*

Her words were slow to come. *You can't promise that. She's vicious.*

I can and I do. I'm coming back to you, today and always.

You'd better...

With Brother Wolf pacing inside him, anxious, ready to break free of Bruno's body, Bruno climbed the stairs, opened the door to the guardhouse, and stared as an all-black wolf with bright violet eyes morphed into a woman he'd never seen before.

CHAPTER FIVE

BRUNO

THE GUARDHOUSE WAS NO LARGER than three by three meters, positioned up high with a long-range view of the entry onto pack land and the surrounding Rocky Mountains. Maverick, Blake, Cleo, Scooby, and a couple of other wolves Bruno hadn't yet met, were crammed into the small room, several of them pointing knives, which were undoubtedly crafted of silver, at the nude woman in the middle of the floor. Albacus and Mordecai floated outside one of several large open windows, peeking their heads inside, Fianna flitting around them incessantly, reminding Bruno of a hummingbird who rarely remained still for long. Or perhaps Clove, though Fianna didn't engender the same desire to clamp onto her shoulders and keep her in place.

Bruno squeezed inside and closed the door behind him, leaning against it.

"Good. You're here," Maverick said, though he didn't remove his gaze from the woman seated on the floor in the middle of the room. His eyes were narrowed with skepticism.

The woman had waist-long, straight, and lustrous black hair that currently hung in front of heavy breasts. She was slim, yet her body wasn't lacking for curves, and her skin was pale and largely unblemished. A single dark beauty mark accentuated one cheekbone. Her mouth was a deep red, her lashes dark and long, which highlighted eyes so violet they seemed unreal.

The woman turned to him. "Bruno," she said, with a familiar, yet subtle, Chinese inflection.

"It's me, Meiling," she said, making Bruno blink at her, though of course he'd already been aware the woman, who must look like Cassia, was claiming to be Naya's identical sister.

And she looked absolutely nothing like her. Their body shapes were perhaps similar, even if Naya was more muscular, but their faces and coloring were nothing alike. Even more, their energy felt different to him, and Brother Wolf reared inside him, alert, aware, and discomfited.

Easy, Bruno told his wolf. His wolf didn't calm in the least.

Maverick said, "She claims that Cassia did something to disconnect her wolf from the moon cycles, so now she can shift at will like a wolf shifter instead of a werewolf, and—"

"Actually," the raven-haired woman corrected, "I said that Cassia had some doctors there that did that."

Maverick gave her a dismissive, *yeah-right* look, and she glared right back at him.

The alpha crossed his arms over his chest. When his muscles bulged, Bruno wondered if he did it as a show of dominance for a woman who could still be more dangerous than all of them combined.

"Then she claims that Cassia gave her some of her immortality magic."

The woman swung her legs to one side for some modesty and readjusted her hair again to cover her breasts. "I'm not claiming anything, that's what she did," the woman said, but her modesty seemed to contradict her statement. Wolves, whether wolf shifters or werewolves, ran around naked as children, and never developed the usual adolescent desire to cover up. Shifters were continually transforming and losing their clothes. Nudity was a way of life for them—for all of them. But it likely wouldn't be for an immortal who wasn't accustomed to shifting her shape.

Meiling should be used to it, even if all she did was transform once a moon cycle.

He allowed his hand to drift toward the silver blade he kept sheathed on his belt.

The woman noticed the subtle movement and rolled her eyes, throwing her hands in the air. "What the...? By the holy book, how am I supposed to convince you that I'm telling the truth? I get that I look like *her*"—her lip curled in disdain, possibly even disgust—"but I'm *not* her."

She sighed, took in a deep breath, and added, "She took me to some place in Southern France. Her doctors have a lab there. They injected me with many unknown substances, linked me up to machines, and studied me. Day and night, they were there, examining me. Next I knew, I could shift at will.

"Then I thought Cassia was going to kiss me. They call her the Kiss of Death, right? So I figured she'd done whatever she wanted to do to me, and that was my end. But instead of killing me, she breathed into me, and next I knew, I almost *did* die. Apparently she shot her magic into me, and it was so strong, my body couldn't take it.

"Her doctors brought me back from near death,

or so they told me. They said I was lucky." She laughed darkly. "As if I wanted her magic inside me." Again, her graceful face puckered in distaste.

"Apparently, the whole idea was to see if her magic could mix with wolf magic."

"To what end?" Bruno asked.

The woman smiled tightly. "Because she just wasn't powerful enough as she was. She wanted to become a wolf shifter as well. And of course she couldn't be bothered to experience the pain of werewolf shifts or to be beholden to the moon cycle. So she waited to see if her people could change that in me before she had me transform her into a wolf."

"Wait, she did what?" Mav asked. "I thought you just said you turned into a shifter. Which shouldn't be possible, actually."

"With magic, anything is possible," Albacus said, a bit too peppily.

"Too true," Mordecai added. "Almost anything, anyway."

"Everything," Albacus amended. "Some things shouldn't be done, but that doesn't mean they can't."

"So you're saying it's possible?" Mav asked them. "To take magic that's natural and occurs without a spell or anything, and change it? Pass it on?"

The wizard brothers looked at each other, bobbing outside the window as they did. Then

Albacus said, "We've never heard of this being done before, but certainly it's possible. In a theoretical manner."

"But theories are merely the ingenuity of persons waiting to be taken from idea," Mordecai said, "to reality." He shrugged, the runes in his pockets jingling mutedly. "So yes, it's possible. Even if we haven't heard of it being done."

The woman nodded eagerly. "I'm telling you, it's true. Why else would I come here?"

"Um, to get to Naya and try to kill her," Blake said.

"*No.* No. I'm here to help Naya. And when I came before, it was only to warn her about Cassia. My ... friend ... Li Kāng, a mage in the Shèng Shān Monastery, found out that I had a sister. He didn't know I had more than one, but he knew a little about Naya and where I might find her."

As one, Maverick and the rest of the Rocky Mountain Pack wolves growled. Bruno snarled just as loudly.

She sighed again, tugging on her hair in frustration. "Listen, I've traveled for weeks to get here. When I escaped, I had no money, documents, or way to contact you. I—" She huffed. "France is a long way away from here when you can't fly like Cassia can."

"So how'd you get here, then?" Maverick asked, a challenging brow arched.

The woman didn't shy away from his stare. "I snuck and I stole from people who didn't deserve it. I killed those who most definitely did deserve it. And I eventually found an animal freighter in Spain, some horse breeders, and I hid on their airplane. They caught me, but not before we landed in Florida."

She paused. "That part isn't important though. I'm here now, *finally*, thank the holy book. I thought Cassia was going to get here before me. But I can feel her now. I can tell where she is. It's as if I can track her." Excitedly, she looked to Maverick. "Like that wolf-head pendant I took from Naya! How would I know that if I'm not who I say I am? Cassia never found out about that."

"That we know of," Maverick said.

She huffed. "How am I going to prove who I am to you if you don't believe anything I say?"

Bruno asked, "Would you believe you if you were in our place?"

Her shoulders slumped, and she rose her knees, folding them against her chest and wrapping her hands around them. "No, I guess I wouldn't. Cassia's plans are pretty insane. She's been planning all this since before we were born."

"How so?" Bruno asked.

The woman hesitated. "Any chance I can wait to tell the full story until Naya's here too? It's ... well ... I'd like her to hear it from me instead of from someone else."

"Not a chance," Mav said. "We don't risk what's most important to us."

The woman nodded and smiled sadly. "I understand. Neither do I."

They all waited, several glancing at Maverick until the woman added in a monotone, "When Cassia got what she wanted from me, she went to kill me." Again, she chuckled darkly. "Because why wouldn't she just kill me like I had no importance? It's how she'd been treating me since before I was even born."

Bruno didn't like the sound of that. He was already tense all over, and now ill ease swept beneath his skin.

"I believed she was going to kill me with that Kiss of Death she does. All the monks in the monastery talk about it. Even the vampire masters do, and they're not scared of anybody, but I think they might be scared of her. Anyway, the *sāobī* leans in, like I said, planning to pull either her immortality magic back out of me, or kill me. I'm not sure which because it was chaos after, and no one stopped to explain anything to me. And *cào*, I don't know which of the two or both she could do."

The woman fiddled with her hair while she continued speaking, splitting it straight down the middle and braiding one of the parts. Bruno's heart slowed as he followed the deft and fast movements of her fingers. Clearly, she'd done this many times before, and no longer cared about modesty. But it was more than that. Bruno had spent time with Meiling while they searched for Naya. And he'd watched her braid her hair on the flight over from Colorado to the Shèng Shān Mountains. Precisely like this. *Exactly* like this. He'd noticed then because he'd never seen anyone complete a braid so quickly and so neatly.

She didn't have anything to tie the end of the braid with when she finished. She glanced at it with a frown, let it fall, then began braiding the second part.

Bruno swallowed, continuing to watch her every movement.

Her frown morphed into a scowl. "They took my hair ribbons. And all my blades. That's so wrong. No one should touch another's weapons. Not unless they're won fair and square in combat. Everyone knows that. *Cào*," she added, with vicious bite. Bruno was no master of any Asian language, but he'd recognize this version of *fuck* regardless.

This sounded like something a warrior would say, who'd been trained in the principles of honorable combat. They didn't, however, sound like the words of an immortal used to taking whatever she wanted, whenever she wanted.

"Whatever Cassia was planning, it failed," the woman said. "She didn't kill me, obviously, though I don't know whether I kept some of her immortality magic or not. I couldn't decide on a safe way to test that."

She pinned Maverick in a fierce look. "I *had* to get back to Naya. And it already took me too long to travel from France to here. The trek was maddeningly slow when I had no ease to help me along. I can't waste any more time. Cassia will be after us. The *sāobī* won't stop until she gets all of us." *Bitch*, Bruno guessed. He'd heard Naya and Clove refer to the immortal that way often enough.

After another meaningful look at Mav, she added, "I have important news to share."

"Then share it," he said.

She shook her head. "You don't believe me ... fine. I suppose. But I'm not telling anyone what I have to say until Naya can hear it too."

"I'm sure we could find a way to motivate you to talk," Mav said, making Bruno twitch uncomfortably. Torture? Was that what the alpha was suggesting?

Bruno was beta of a wolf pack. He was under no delusions about the steps sometimes needed to survive in a world where they were always hunted, and by an organized and well-funded force no less. Too often, the ends justified the means out of necessity.

But this might be Meiling...

But then, it still could be Cassia, deceiving them all. Who was to say an immortal who'd lived more than a thousand years wouldn't be an astute study of character? She might be fully capable of studying Meiling and learning her mannerisms and accent. Hadn't the woman even pretty much admitted that she was a science experiment?

But the woman appeared less concerned by Maverick's threat than Bruno. Without blinking, she pinned him in a steady stare. "I've lived my entire life in the Shèng Shān Monastery. Before traveling to warn Naya, I trained every single day of my life that I can remember. From sunup to sundown. The vampire masters are unforgiving, unrelenting, vicious, and cruel. They demand us to give what no one can give for long without losing a part of themselves. Their humanity. I probably would have lost mine if not for the fact that I was the only werewolf among them."

Her stare hardened further. "If the master

vampires didn't manage to break me over nearly twenty-three years, you won't achieve it either."

Bruno might not have decided whether or not he believed her, but he didn't doubt her in this. From the resigned line of Maverick's mouth, he didn't think he doubted her conviction either.

Finally, the woman nodded and arranged the tidy weave of her braids across her breasts, where they concealed nothing. She no longer appeared concerned, however.

Sitting on the floor as she was, she stared off between the legs of those surrounding her, her eyes losing focus.

"All I know for certain is that Cassia tried to do something to me, to neutralize me, and it didn't go as the *sāobī* planned. Somehow, for whatever reason, we switched bodies. Everyone there was as surprised as I was, and Cassia most of all. She became very upset and ran out of the lab.

"No one seemed to know what to do. Not her scientists, not that subservient vampire Édouard who follows her everywhere like he's her pet—I killed him. And certainly not the other vampires who follow him around, afraid of Cassia's shadow.

"None of them expected me to survive. No one thought she'd run off without giving final orders. I think maybe none of them even expected it to work.

But I saw her shift into a wolf before she left, so even though they somehow disconnected me from the moon, and I can now shift at will, I still passed on the wolf magic like a werewolf."

She shrugged. "I didn't know what to do. All I knew was that I was still alive, Cassia looked like me, and she was now a wolf. And probably also an immortal, I don't know. When I had my chance to escape, I did, making sure to head in the opposite direction of Cassia's scent. Since then, I've been making my way here. And that's it. Until I can see Naya."

The woman didn't shy away from staring down Maverick, even though the shifter was pulsing alpha power throughout the room, making some of his wolves bow their heads to him and keep their gazes lowered in deference.

Scowling furiously, arms still crossed, Maverick looked every bit the ferocious alpha shifter capable of defending his pack and the treasure they concealed within it.

After staring at her for an entire minute, he looked at the mages behind her. "Is this really possible? Could she be telling the truth?"

"Yes and yes," Mordecai said, uncommonly succinct. "Probably, I don't know, but possible, definitely."

Mav faced Bruno. "What do you think? You're mate to her supposed sister."

Bruno didn't think he knew, and was opening his mouth to say so when he noticed Brother Wolf had settled inside him somewhere along the course of her story. His wolf wasn't behaving as if the woman were a threat to his mate. Not at all. Brother Wolf was curled up into a tight ball at his center, at ease but for the fact that he yearned to return to Naya.

"*Dios*," Bruno whispered. "It's true." Awe had him shaking his head. "I can't believe it."

"I can't either," Mav muttered. "What makes you believe her?"

"My wolf. He trusts her."

Silence filled the room until all that stood out were the calls of forest birds and the soft buzzing of Fianna's wings.

"Damn," Mav eventually muttered, shattering the silence. "There's no way Cassia could fool your wolf, not when you're mate to her sister. To her twin."

"Even if they don't look like twins anymore," Mordecai interjected.

"Or even sisters, really," Albacus said.

"Her internal energy *should* remain the same."

Albacus nodded, his beard and hair tinkling. "It should indeed."

"Should?" Maverick asked.

"Well, there are no certainties in magic, only possibilities," Mordecai said.

"And this is more potent—" Albacus said.

"And rarer."

"And rarer magic than most," Albacus added. "If the wolf within Naya's mate believes this is her true sister, it's highly likely it is."

"Highly likely?" Mav repeated.

The mages nodded their heads, making them look so similar as their gestures were nearly identical. With their long gray hair and equally long beards, matching robes, and similar quirky personalities, they might have been twins themselves.

Mav shook his head. "If there's even a chance you're actually Cassia, I can't do it. I won't. I won't risk Naya."

The woman stood, causing everyone there, save the wizards and Bruno, to tense in readiness for an attack. Weapons extended, muscles tightened, and low growls rumbled through the small space.

"You don't want to take the chance?" the woman asked, walking until she stood arm's length from the alpha. "I understand. I wouldn't want to risk Naya either if the circumstances were reversed. But you're going to have to take the small chance that I'm somehow deceiving a wolf who would always know and be able to cut through any lie."

"And why would I risk Naya? After all I've done to protect her during the course of her entire life? When her most dangerous enemy might be standing in front of me?"

"Because, to keep her fully safe, you need the information I possess, and I'll only share it with her."

The alpha and the woman stared each other down. Then the woman softened, her face relaxing into a tentative, hopeful smile.

"Besides, I promise on my life, which might be immortal now, I don't know, never to hurt my sister."

At that, Bruno's eyes widened, and he asked the wizards, "Even if my wolf were deceived, and this were actually Cassia, could an immortal with unknown magic be bound to a promise not to hurt Naya, no matter what?"

The brothers smiled, cutting through all that facial hair.

"Oh yes," Albacus said.

Mordecai's face stretched further into a grin. "Definitely."

CHAPTER SIX

BRUNO

BRUNO UPDATED Naya via their mate bond while he half listened to the conversations taking place around him. The wizard brothers discussed which of several oath spells they should use to guarantee the best results, given the unknown scope of Meiling's newfound magic—or possibly Cassia's.

Despite the ease of Bruno's wolf around the woman, Maverick remained dubious, a fact he didn't bother hiding, glaring openly at the woman as if the force of his stare alone would kill her if she were deceiving them.

While the argument between the mages became heated, and Mordecai threatened to consult his runes, causing Albacus to wave his hands in front of his face, loudly protesting the waste of time, Cleo and Scooby talked of the woman's wolf.

They'd seen Meiling shift when the full moon claimed her at the base of Shèng Shān Mountain, but she'd only completed a partial transformation when Cassia snatched her away. Meiling's wolf had been black then too. But while a black wolf was uncommon in a wolf shifter, it wasn't entirely unheard of. And while the woman's wolf *did* match what parts Cleo and Scooby had witnessed when they were still certain the beast belonged to the true Meiling, it was possible, though implausible, that Cassia's wolf might possess an identical physical appearance, especially as the women had presumedly swapped bodies.

Basically, we know fuck-all, Naya summarized through their link. *But if you believe her, so do I. I want to see her.*

Right now, Mav looks like he might tear her head off before he lets her come within a hundred meters of you.

Great. There's no way he's gonna let me see her, then.

He's thinking about it though. He has to be.

If this is really Meiling, and she has information that could protect me from the real Cassia ... he's stuck between a rock and an even fucking harder rock.

Yes, he is.

But he'd better not hurt her trying to get the info out of her. He can't risk harming Meiling.

I think he'd try it if he thought she'd talk, but she was pretty convincing when she told him the only way he was finding out what she knew was if he let her see you.

Sounds like Meiling.

It did to me too. Oh, wait. It looks like the mages came to a decision.

"It's the very large blue book," Albacus was telling the very un-large fairy, who was apparently expected to retrieve said book and deliver it to them. "It's at the Magical Arts Academy, in our personal library. On the, hmm, ah, third shelf from the top, next to the entryway."

"Fourth shelf, brother," Mordecai corrected.

"Third," Albacus said.

"Fourth."

Fianna smiled tightly. "I'll check both the third *and* fourth shelves, don't you worry." She was obviously accustomed to intervening between them. "What's the title of the book?"

"Oh." Albacus actually giggled, and once more he sounded delighted by life and its constant adventures. "Of course you'll need that. There are quite a few sizable blue books in our collection. Especially when one takes into account the vast range in hues of the color blue." Which Bruno wasn't.

Albacus added, "This one is *Advanced Spells for Rare, Uncommon, and Bizarrely Strange Magic.*"

Mordecai added, "The gilding on the title is a bit worn. The book is older than we are."

"It belonged to our parents, and perhaps even to our ancestors before them."

"But you'll be able to find it," Mordecai said.

"I'm sure I will." Fianna buzzed closer, landing to rest on the windowsill. "Anything else?"

"That's it," Albacus said.

Fianna the Crimson dipped her head. "Then I'm off. Remember, the farther the physical distance, the longer it will take me to travel. But I'll be back as soon as I can."

A very loud pop, which made Brother Wolf wince, signaled her sudden departure. She was there one moment, gone the next.

"How long will she take?" Mav asked the wizards.

"Fifteen minutes." Mordecai shrugged. "Maybe as much as an hour."

An hour? Naya groaned after Bruno relayed the news. *I'm gonna have to tackle Clove to the ground by then. If not, River might, and I don't think that'll go as well. Though, Clove might actually like that. One of her first crushes was on River.*

To keep her from wrestling her best friend into stillness, Bruno said, *I received a letter from Lara.*

That's what Theo wanted with you earlier at the gym?

I didn't know that was his name, but sí. He paused. *She's ordered me to return.*

Naya's response arrived right away. *But you can't. Not yet. Not without me.*

His words were soft, though his initial reaction to the letter's contents had been as forceful as hers. *I know. And don't worry, I'm not going anywhere without you. Not now, not ever.*

Even if it means disobeying your alpha?

She'll understand. But would she? Lara *was* understanding, and he even considered her a friend, or as much of one as an alpha would allow herself to be to one of her pack wolves. But she was still his alpha, which meant that he was expected to obey any command she gave. And not just expected, *required.*

We'll figure it out, he said, though he had no idea how to balance his responsibilities as beta and a pack wolf of the Andes Mountain Pack with his duty as mate to one of the most important werewolves on the entire planet.

As if Naya were also considering the impossible

situation in which he found himself, she was quiet, until, *Have the wizards said what they wanted with me when Fianna came to fetch me?*

No, but their plans seem to change all the time. Not that I can blame them. We don't know exactly what we're working with, and the situation keeps changing on them.

Shifters typically stored spare clothing all over pack territory. Cleo rummaged in some drawers and emerged with clothing for the nude woman, who tipped her head in gratitude before stepping into clothes that were several sizes too big for her, clearly meant for a large man. Standing within the loose, draping fabric, she seemed small and inoffensive.

Bruno wasn't fooled by appearances, however.

Even if this were actually Meiling and not Cassia, Meiling was a trained warrior, capable of killing with her bare hands, despite her penchant for shiny knives.

Fully dressed, the dark-haired woman walked toward him.

Hold on, amor. *She's coming to speak with me now,* Bruno told Naya, before smiling tightly, offering the woman only a slight welcome.

She asked, "How's Naya? Is she ... I haven't been able to stop thinking about her. She was with Cassia for so long."

Before answering, Bruno shot a look at Maverick, who delayed, but finally nodded. "But no details. Not until we confirm who she really is. We play our cards close to the vest."

The woman turned toward the alpha. "If you can suggest a way I can irrevocably prove myself to you, let me know and I'll do it."

Bruno took her arm. "Come, let's sit. It's too cramped in here." As he led her out onto the narrow wraparound perimeter to the lookout, Mav said, "Go no farther."

Bruno wasn't planning on it.

The dark-haired woman Bruno hoped was actually Meiling slid to the ground and leaned her head back against the wooden planks, closing her eyes. Like this, unguarded, she seemed exhausted. If her story was true, she had reason to be. "Just tell me she's all right."

Bruno hesitated, unsure what, if anything, he should tell this woman before the wizards could perform their binding spell.

Maybe-Meiling pinned Bruno in a stare, and he caught a flash of desperation in those odd, disturbingly violet eyes. "Please," she said. "She's my sister. I only just found her. I can't bear the thought of losing her." She paused. "She is okay, isn't she? Did...?" She swallowed hard. "Did Cassia hurt her?"

Brother Wolf whined, as if to urge Bruno to answer her, to assure Naya's sister that his mate was well. Recovered. Safe.

Bruno forced himself to relax, breathing deeply. "She *was* badly hurt," he said softly. "And..." He struggled to get the words out. He hardly allowed himself to think of it. "She died."

Likely-Meiling sucked in a choppy breath. "She ... died? Oh no. Is, *cào*, tell me already, Bruno! Unless this is some kind of torture Mav's put you up to, and in that case, keep going, because it's working."

Bruno faced her, patting her arm to calm her surge of panic.

"She's fine now. But I wasn't sure she would be for long enough to age me a hundred years." He hadn't aged a day in actuality, but his heart felt heavy with all he now had to lose.

"I understand that," Almost-Certainly-Meiling said. "You don't know what it's been like since I last saw you. It's been..." She shook her head, strands of dark hair escaping the braids she hadn't managed to tie off. "I grew up under the constant weight of vampire masters, who are nearly as horrible as Cassia. But I got used to it. We all had to in order to survive. I'm not used to being scared anymore. But Cassia? Cassia scares me."

"She sounds terrifying. No one should murder without reason, for power, for display."

"No, no one should." Her lips settled into a determined line. If Meiling was in there, Cassia had made a true enemy of her.

The woman crossed her legs into lotus position and appeared to reassuringly pat where a blade usually strapped to her thigh. She cracked her knuckles when she came up empty, pointing her stare up at the faded wood of the wraparound's ceiling.

"How did Naya die?"

That likely fell into Mav's "unnecessary details" restriction, but Bruno answered anyway. "She climbed down the back of Shèng Shān Mountain, trying to escape Cassia."

Definitely-Meiling blinked and turned her entire body toward him. "She did *what*?"

"She says it was either that or die, and she ended up dying anyway, at least for a while. Long enough to make Brother Wolf go absolutely crazy." The man had suffered as much, if not more, but Bruno didn't say that. Any wolf shifter, even if she'd started out in life as a werewolf, would know that.

"No one's *ever* tried that climb," Meiling said. "Not even when they knew the vampires were going to kill them. No one can make it down that bald rock face. No one."

"Your sister can."

Meiling shook her head. "That's..." She whistled under her breath. "That's impressive. Crazy!"

"It is. It was."

"I knew she could climb. She told me she was good. But that's not just good, that's..."

"That's inhumanly good. And she climbed down barefoot and without any gear."

"I have no words for how incredible she is."

He smiled, feeling more relaxed now that each new exchange further convinced him she was who she claimed to be. "She is pretty spectacular," he said. "She only fell when her wolf came over her, and by then she was almost down. We think she fell like two hundred feet. Maybe more."

"And she came out of it." Again, she shook her head in disbelief. "I don't think Cassia knows. I don't know why, but she thought Naya was me."

Bruno cast a glance toward the wall, and the warning alpha growl drifting through the open window. Bruno said, "I'll let Naya catch you up on everything after the wizards do their binding spell."

She sighed in resignation. "Understood. At least she's okay now. She fully recovered?"

"Other than a scar, yes."

"A scar?" Another shake of the head. "It must've been really bad, then."

"It was. The scar is long."

She brought a hand to her eyes. "To think, my actions might've killed her for real." Another growl from Maverick and also Blake. "I set off to warn her and keep her safe—" Another set of condemning growls. She ignored them. "And then she ended up at the monastery, taking my place."

"Hey," Bruno said. "No one's to blame here but Cassia."

"Yes," she said, but she didn't sound convinced. Then, "Cassia's been behind all this for longer than we realized."

"Right. It seems she's the one who delivered you to your packs, or monastery, as infants."

She offered him a regretful smile. "I'd tell you more, Bruno, really I would. But then I'd lose my leverage, and the alpha in there might cut me into many small pieces just for looking like the wrong person."

Mierda. He'd really wished she'd tell him. But she did have a point.

"What's it like?" he asked. "Looking like her?"

Meiling's face transformed. Its alluring curves pressed into bitter lines; even the bright violet of her eyes seemed to darken.

"It's awful. She's horrible. Does horrible things. And now I'll forever be reminded of her every time I look into a mirror, or see hands that don't look like mine. Each time I see any part of my body it feels foreign."

She smoothed out her eyebrows as if she could smooth out her physical discomfort. "Don't get me wrong. I'm grateful to be alive, especially so I can pass on what I learned to Naya, and I guess also you. Lara needs to know everything as well. I wasn't ready to die. I didn't survive twenty-two years in that monastery hell just to have Cassia take me down now. And if I actually have immortality magic, that could be nice. Maybe. I haven't decided yet. I, well, I want to look like me. Like my sisters. Now that I've finally learned I have them, now I'm the outside one. I'm the only one who won't look like them anymore."

"I don't think they'll see you as the outside one."

She shrugged. "They might not want to, but they may not be able to help it. Especially not Naya. She's been around Cassia when she looked like this." Meiling ran a hand along the length of her body. "It'd be hard not to associate what she sees with Cassia."

"You should give Naya more credit." Though Meiling did have a point. People didn't always react the way they wanted to, and Naya had experienced trauma at the hands of the immortal.

Meiling rubbed at her knees and smiled sadly. "I can't change it either way. I don't know how." She perked up. "Maybe Albacus or Mordecai will."

"Maybe. But don't get your hopes up. They haven't been able to decide on much when it comes to Cassia. She's too much of an unknown."

"Yes, she is. And she's incredibly dangerous. And also likely insane too. I hope that fairy hurries. I shouldn't keep to myself what I know for long."

Then don't, Bruno wanted to say, but she was right. It was her only leverage, and Bruno was convinced now this was Meiling.

"Hey, um." Meiling massaged her calves, not meeting Bruno's eye. "Did Naya happen to mention my friend Li Kāng to you?"

"She did."

She glanced over at him. "And?"

"I'll let her tell you everything."

"Is he alive?"

"I'm sorry, Mei, but I really don't know. When Naya last saw him, he was fighting Cassia. Alone."

She nodded absently, eyes blank and suddenly shiny.

This was Meiling. Bruno didn't believe Cassia capable of this kind of emotion, not even as an act.

"I'm sorry," Bruno said. "She can tell you more."

Another distracted nod from Meiling before a

pop shattered the crisp mountain air once more, leaving Bruno's ears ringing.

Meiling sniffled, stood, and straightened her shoulders, before marching back inside, where the diminutive fairy was busy removing a matchbook-sized book from the folds of her gauzy, tutu-like scarlet skirt.

She flew down to set the tiny volume on the floor before unfolding it once, doubling it in size. She unfolded it again, and again, and another time still, until the dusty blue and faded volume was many times larger than she was.

The book was as long as Bruno's arm and as thick as his hand. Fianna was panting by the time she revealed its full and original size.

She wiped her forehead. "There. Now I need a nap. And a raise. Getting that off the shelf was not fun. At all."

Albacus and Mordecai, who'd floated inside to half sit, half hovered next to the book on the floor, both looked at her.

"Was it on the third shelf like Albacus said, or was it actually on the fourth shelf, where it always is?" Mordecai asked.

Fianna tsked, cocked a hip out, and wagged her finger at Mordecai. "You know I don't pick sides."

Mordecai's face drooped into feigned innocence,

a look he didn't pull off. "I'm not asking you to pick sides. I'm just asking you to report back the truth. Your experience is all. Nothing more."

"Mm-hmm." She lathered on the sarcasm. Mordecai only pushed the extent of his supposed innocence, his smile frozen in place.

"Oh, stop pestering her, brother," Albacus said. "You know she'll tell you if you push her enough, no matter what she says now. So don't push her. She's just trying to protect your ego."

"My ego?" All traces of innocence evaporated from the wizard's translucent face.

"Yes," Albacus said. "The book was definitely on the third shelf. It's written all over the lovely Fianna's face."

"Now you're brown-nosing!" Mordecai accused.

Albacus' head whipped back in affront. "I am *not*. And what a disgusting saying. Not one of the finest inventions of the previous century."

Maverick growled the way adult wolves did when disciplining pups. The mages quieted, each attempting nonchalance, and failing.

"What else do you need to perform the spell that will enforce the woman's promise not to harm Naya?" Mav asked, his question a gruff rumble that agitated Bruno's own wolf.

Albacus and Mordecai exchanged a look.

"Nothing," Albacus said.

"Then I suggest you get to it. I'm not known for my patience."

Bruno didn't know of a wolf shifter who was.

Albacus cleared his throat. "Everyone but Meiling, step back."

They pressed themselves against the walls, then watched in amazement as the translucent half-alive wizards, who floated through walls, managed to touch the solid book and flip its pages.

Those two were walking, talking—very loquaciously—contradictions.

Peligrosa, the mages are starting the spell now. I'll bring Meiling to you soon.

Thank fuck, Naya said right away. *A fight broke loose over here.*

Clove?

Yup. Had to keep a few wolves from throttling her. Soon can't come fast enough.

Brother Wolf agreed. Already he longed to return to his mate.

He had to keep her safe.

Always.

CHAPTER SEVEN

NAYA

THE WIZARDS' oath spell was a success, so Mav was escorting Meiling home. Nervous anticipation raced through her, making it even harder than before to wait. But she didn't move from the center of the protective circle where her alpha had ordered her to stay. Not even when there were signs everywhere of the scuffle that had taken place in his absence.

Clove sat on the ground beside her, in the middle of a patch of torn-up grass, finally still. Her hair stood up in all directions from when Kady, a willowy yet fierce shifter raised in the Bronx, told Clove she'd "beat the shit out of her if she didn't sit her ass the fuck down already." Clove's reply had been a simple "Fuck you very much, Kady."

Kady proceeded to tackle Clove to the ground

with an inhuman roar, and River hadn't lifted a finger to intervene for longer than was necessary.

Afterward, Clove pouted, even though she'd held her own, as Naya knew she would. Before long, however, Clove grew pleased with herself, a fact that made Kady resume her threats.

Meiling couldn't arrive soon enough.

How long? Naya asked Bruno.

Almost there.

Clove's shirt was torn, her elbows and knees stained green and brown, and two of her belt loops dangled from the waistband of her jeans.

Naya offered her a hand up. "They'll be here in a minute."

Clove glared up at her. "Took you long enough to have my back."

"You're lucky I jumped in at all. I'm pretty sure every single one of us here wanted to yank your hair out before Kady did."

None of the dozens of wolves surrounding them corrected Naya.

Clove's stare never moved from her. "I don't care about the others. But *you* saying that? Damn, Ni, that stings. I thought we were sisters."

"Of course we're sisters. We'll always be sisters. It's just, do you have to go out of your way to drive us all nuts? Aren't we nuts enough without that? We're all tense as mofos right now with what's going on. We're riding the motherfucking edge, dammit. Can't you tell?"

Of course she could.

"Why do you think—?"

But River cut her off. "They're here."

As one, every shifter turned to watch their alpha and his entourage approach.

Even with Bruno alongside Mav, Naya couldn't tear her attention away from the woman with the jet-black hair and violet eyes.

Cassia.

Her heartbeat sped up, her breathing came faster, and she had to resist the overwhelming urge to throw herself at the woman and find the way to kill her. Immortal or not, she needed to *die*.

Naya didn't even notice when Clove rose, but suddenly she was beside her, once more holding her hand. "It's okay, Ni. It's not really her, remember? It just looks like her."

Naya barely registered Clove's reassurance. Sister Wolf was fighting to break free, and Naya couldn't recall exactly why she shouldn't let her wolf have at the immortal who'd done nothing but hurt people—who held her sister.

"Take in deep breaths, girl," Clove said, rubbing her back.

But Naya didn't fucking feel like focusing on her breath. She wanted to dismember the bitch with those cool, calm, merciless eyes. They didn't even look real with their odd coloring.

Then Bruno was on her other side; she hadn't noticed him move. He spoke to her through their private link.

It's not Cassia. It's Meiling. I'm sure of it, peligrosa.

It was his nickname for her that finally broke past her instincts to her rational mind.

She blinked, then dragged her gaze up and down the woman who now stood a body length away from her, armed wolves on all sides, Maverick practically standing on top of her despite the mages' reassurance that Meiling couldn't hurt Naya if she happened to be deceiving them all.

Amor, don't look with your eyes. Use your other senses.

She processed Bruno's advice and realized he was probably right. But she couldn't get her nostrils to stop flaring, her jaw to relax, or her fingers to stop wanting to punish the woman for her thousand years of killing and maiming and destroying families and bonds, of raining fear and pain and devastation.

She was the Kiss of Death.

Why did someone like her get to have eternal

life? Why someone so incredibly unworthy of the gift?

"Naya, it's me, Meiling," the woman said in a soft, imploring tone that suggested Naya was a wild, unpredictable animal.

Her voice was Cassia's, but with Meiling's understated Chinese lilt. When the woman laughed nervously, Naya realized she'd never heard Cassia laugh. The sound reminded her of her sister.

"I understand how strange it is to see me in her body." Another strained chuckle. "Trust me, I can barely stand seeing myself like this. But she was trying to kill me when"—she gestured up and down her body with both hands—"*this* happened, so I guess I'm lucky. Maybe." She grimaced. "I'm avoiding mirrors for now."

Naya stared at her some more. The long black hair, violet eyes, and beautiful supermodel face were all Cassia. Not even the baggy sweatpants and over-sized t-shirt could fully conceal the sensual curves that swept across all the right places.

But her stance...

Cassia walked as if she were a sleek, sensuous jungle cat, always one lunge away from attack no matter what she was doing. Normally, even when Cassia attempted to come off as innocuous, she failed to disguise her predatory nature. But this woman, this Cassia, stood with a different kind of strength, muscles loose and relaxed, back straight, knees unlocked.

Like a martial artist.

Naya couldn't even tell all that made her distinguish the gait and posture from Cassia's, but she was certain of the difference.

This was how Meiling stood and walked, even if this new body lacked her many years of training and muscle memory.

"I'd offer to let you test me somehow," the woman said, appearing almost sheepish as she tilted her head downward, "but I'm not sure there's anything you could ask me that would do it." She cast a meaningful look at Mav, before pinning her stare back on Naya. "If she can infiltrate our minds, there's nothing I know that she couldn't have potentially accessed."

"*Did* she get in your head?" Maverick asked from behind her.

While meeting the same question in Naya's eyes, the woman said, "No, I don't think so. But..." She sighed loudly, heavily, resignedly. "I can't be sure of it. There were days where I was in so much pain and completely out of my body, my mind too, thinking I was going to die, that I don't think I would've realized if she were in there, poking around."

"So you could be compromised," Mav said on a growl.

"She isn't," Albacus said as he and his brother floated closer. "We checked."

"You checked?" Mav asked. "Without my permission?"

Albacus shrugged despite the dangerous edge to the alpha's questions. "We didn't think you'd mind us taking steps to keep your pack members safe."

Mav frowned, but didn't retort.

Mordecai smoothed a hand down the length of his beard. "We can't be fully certain Cassia was never in there, but she isn't in Meiling's mind now."

"And she's left no back doors for herself to get back in," Albacus said, anticipating Mav's next question.

"It's probably because she planned to kill me," the woman said. "She didn't expect the body exchange to happen. She was as stunned by it as I was—and let me tell you, I was *shocked*. I did not anticipate that. Even her vampire slaves didn't know what to do. Everyone just froze. And then"—a shrug —"she took off. She ran off as a wolf and didn't come back. Her vampire butler, or whatever he was, tried to kill me, but I did him the favor first, with his own silver sword. Then I got the hell out of there and began the long, arduous journey here."

"They just ... let you go?" River asked, sounding as dubious as Naya felt. "They didn't have you tied down or anything?"

"Oh they did. The straps were woven through with silver too. But I didn't train all my life in Seimei Do to let a few bindings stop me. Not when I finally had my chance to escape."

Clove released her hand, but Naya still wasn't sure she could trust the woman, no matter how she stood, no matter what she said.

Sister Wolf didn't trust her.

Violet Eyes took another step toward her, and tension crackled through the air like a whip. The woman tensed but didn't acknowledge the fact that obviously no one trusted her.

"Naya, please. I won't ask you to trust me, because I understand that's pointless. I know as well as you that Cassia is fully capable of planning this whole act just to get to you. But, well, I need to know."

Those violet eyes welled with what Naya thought might be fear. "Bruno told me when you last saw Li Kāng he was fighting Cassia? Alone?"

That's when Naya's Sister Wolf calmed. That's when Naya knew. The love and concern and hope and devastation that shone through those violet eyes were emotions the real Cassia wasn't capable of mimicking. The real Cassia had forgotten how to care about anyone but herself.

She exhaled deeply and felt the stress melt from her body. She leaned into Bruno's hand at her back, finding simple comfort in his closeness.

"I'm so sorry, Mei, but I don't know. I don't know if he survived or not. But he's the reason I'm here now. He told me he loved you, all but shoved me out the window, and did what he could to hold her off."

Meiling's back stiffened and she pointed her chin up. Tears pooled at the rim of her bottom eyelid. Her lips pressed together firmly and she nodded several times. When she sniffed, Naya took a step toward her.

Meiling held up a hand, keeping her at bay. All eyes were on her.

She said, "Then he died as bravely as he lived. He's the only reason I found out about you in the first place. He's how I managed to escape and come to you. He was the best kind of ... friend."

Naya took another step forward, but Mei only sniffed again, swiped at her eyes, and announced, "I have important news to share with you, and you're not going to like it." She looked at Mav. "Any chance I can talk to Naya in private?"

"None."

"You want me to tell her everything here, in front of everyone? This is unexpected ... news."

Maverick hesitated as the attention of his pack wolves landed on him. If he told her not to share, he'd be openly keeping secrets from them, and while they all knew he didn't share everything with them—no alpha did—trust was an essential part of the contract between alpha and pack shifter.

"Tell us," Mav finally said.

Meiling sighed. "Very well." She studied the large group huddled around them for a few moments, before locking eyes with Naya and not letting go.

"There aren't three of us, there are four of us."

A four-ton boulder pressed against Naya's chest. "What?"

"Not three sisters, but four." A sad smile. "Or anyway, there were four of us."

Naya swallowed, her brows drawing together. "Were?" She eked the word out.

"Yes, *were*. Cassia got to Davina first."

"Davina," Naya repeated, testing out the name.

Meiling nodded. "From what I gathered, Cassia did to her what she did to me, only her scientists hadn't figured things out as well as they had when she brought me in. I heard the scientists talking, and they said Davina died after Cassia shared a small part of her immortality magic with her. Like she did with me."

"Fuck," Clove whispered in horror from beside Naya.

"Yes." Meiling frowned. "We had another sister, identical to us, and now we'll never get to meet her."

A pit the size of a lakebed opened up in Naya's stomach. Sister Wolf threw back her head and howled a lament as sad as any funeral dirge—at the loss of a connection she hadn't known she had but now desperately needed.

A sister she'd never know. Never touch. Never hear.

After an entire minute, during which no one said anything, as if honoring the memory of a woman they should have all known, Meiling asked, "Ready for the rest of the news? It's just as bad."

"Oh my God, how could it be?" Clove ground out, speaking Naya's exact thoughts aloud. "There was another heir to Callan 'the Oak' MacLeod, another chance to save werewolves, and the fucking bitch just killed her?"

"Cassia," Meiling said, "has been lying to us all this time. To everyone." Meiling glanced at Maverick. "Especially to you." She looked at Bruno. "And to your pack too."

Naya's throat was suddenly so dry she couldn't remember the last time she'd drunk water.

Lies? What lies?

"Cassia took advantage of a husband and wife desperate to have children, and arranged everything until the wife was pregnant with the four of us. In vitro, the best science had to offer. Cassia had a hand in making us before we even existed."

Naya couldn't move a muscle. All she could do was wait for the rest, already anticipating her entire world was about to shatter—nothing would be the same after she heard the rest. Dread pulsed inside her as if it were her very heartbeat.

"Cassia wants—wanted, because she got her wish —to be a wolf shifter. Apparently being an immortal wasn't enough for her. But she didn't want to be a werewolf and have to go through painful shifts and be tied to the moon." She paused, and the silence nearly crackled with tension. "She bred the four of us to be her lab experiments. She found a team of experts to figure out how to get one of us to pass on werewolf magic, but then have it adjusted so she could become a wolf shifter."

Even the forest that surrounded them quieted while Meiling spoke.

"That whole story we were all told about Callan

'the Oak' MacLeod? Heirs to the ancestral bloodline? Bullshit. Total and absolute bullshit."

"But..." Maverick said. "But the werewolves are declining. It's true that there are less and less of them in the world, that less new werewolves are able to withstand the intensity of werewolf magic and survive their first shifts."

"I don't know about that," Meiling said. "Maybe werewolves are dying out naturally and she used that fact to make her story believable. I don't know. But what I do know from Cassia, who told me this directly, is that she fabricated this whole tale so we'd all remain alive and protected. So her 'experiments' would survive until she deemed us strong enough to experiment on. Until our magic was powerful enough to pass on to her."

A bird chirped and it made Naya jump, yanking her out of her stupor. "It can't be," she whispered.

"But it is. She impregnated our mother, then killed our parents, separated us to increase our chances at survival since hunters are a real thing, then fed everyone these lies so we'd live until we were ripe for harvesting."

Naya didn't even feel her legs buckle, but suddenly Bruno was guiding her down to the ground.

Her entire life ... a prisoner of her destiny ...

never allowed to leave pack territory ... to choose a damn thing about her own life...

Meiling flexed her fingers at her sides, patting her legs in a gesture that Naya thought meant she was reaching for weapons she no longer wore. "The worst part about it all is we can't even kill her. We can't make her pay for all she's done."

"We've been thinking about that," Albacus said, glancing at Mordecai before studying Naya and Meiling, and landing on Meiling.

"You do have immortality magic."

"Not as much as Cassia," Mordecai said, "but it should be enough."

"For what?" Maverick asked, his voice murderous, his eyes a single glow of gold. River and Blake walked to his side as warrior energy rolled off him so thickly the entire pack would be feeling it.

"We have an idea," Albacus said.

"And now that Naya and Meiling aren't saviors that can't be touched," Mordecai said, "it's a manageable risk."

"Manageable risk? Like hell it is," Bruno said, his pack magic's green overcoming his eyes.

"You might not like it, but it's a plan," Albacus said. "If Meiling can track Cassia, we can find her, and use her immortality magic against her."

"Okay," Maverick said. "Tell us more."

"The girls might look different now," Mordecai said, "but their energy signature will still be that of identical twins."

"And?" Maverick's question was a low, dangerous, lethal grumble.

"We merge their energies," Albacus said. "With two of them possessing immortality magic, we double our chances at them drawing Cassia's out of her."

"We think it's the only way to kill her," Albacus said.

"I don't care. It's not happening," Maverick said.

"But…" the brothers protested at the same time.

"But nothing. We're done here."

He stalked off, River and Blake on either side of him. Over his shoulder, he called, "Naya, Bruno, Meiling, you're with me." With a snarl, "Albacus and Mordecai too."

Then, through the pack link that broadcast to the nearly thousand wolves of the Rocky Mountain Pack combined, he said, *Prepare. We're going to war.*

Finally, a command Naya could get behind.

CHAPTER EIGHT

CASSIA

DAYS AND NIGHTS HAD PASSED, but Cassia didn't know how many. She hadn't bothered counting the sunsets or sunrises. What did they matter anymore? As she trekked across forests, the usual painful weight of outliving everyone she knew was nothing compared to the image of Édouard dying in her arms. She'd endure beyond even the lifespans of the tall, overarching trees that shaded her path—but who fucking cared? That ungrateful *puttana* Meiling had taken what was *hers*. *She* was the only one who got to decide what happened to Édouard. He was *her* servant, the most dedicated one she'd ever had. He was irreplaceable! Cassia could buy another thousand vapid vampires and none of them would fulfill her wishes with the dedication Édouard had.

LUCÍA ASHTA

Cassia was going to murder Meiling. The only question left was how long she'd make her suffer before she delighted in watching her shrivel into an empty skin sack. If the idiot girl thought what Cassia had done to her Master Xiong was bad, it was nothing compared to how long Cassia would punish her.

It had been a long while since Cassia felt the need to be creative in her kills. No torment would be sufficient for the girl. Cassia would end her in such a way that the entire community of werewolves would suffer nightmares splattered in blood.

She bared her teeth, snarling loudly into the crisp woodland that surrounded her. Birds high up in the trees, out of her reach, scattered in a loud flap of agitated wings.

That's right. *Flee while you still can,* Cassia projected to Meiling, her thoughts always on the girl, most sounds, smells, and urges tangling with her desire to bring her to her knees. *There's no place you can go where I won't find you, you fucking little brat.*

Like a coward, Meiling had fled with some of her immortality magic. Cassia would be having that back, *grazie,* before she flayed the flesh from her bones, savoring her pained screams.

The other girls she'd bred ... Cassia had thought that maybe, after all her efforts in bringing them into

108

existence and then keeping them alive all these years, it would be better to allow them to survive in case something changed. If she was an apex predator now, what could she become with more changes? What might it feel like to be, say, a bear shifter? All that strength and power? That magnificent size?

But now she wouldn't allow a single one of those bitches to live. They'd all pay for Meiling's sins. Cassia would visit proper payment on each and every one of them. Meiling would die knowing she was responsible for every one of their pained cries, for every plea for mercy Cassia wouldn't heed.

Her lips stretched back across her muzzle to reveal a wicked grin. Before her first shift, she'd left orders for Édouard to kill Kirill and the least useful of the scientists. She'd planned to keep Doctor Patel and a couple of the others, just in case she needed them again. She'd pay them well enough to keep their mouths shut, and if they didn't, well, Édouard had his orders.

Everything had been taken care of. Édouard was to be her eyes and ears while she was absent enjoying the fruits of her labor, experiencing the glory of this new beast she inhabited. If any threats arose, he was to contain them and inform her. Eventually. When she finally made contact again. She was supposed to be in no hurry to reconnect with the human side of her life.

Meiling had fucked all that up, every one of her plans, and her ability to enjoy her wolf without tainting the experience with thoughts of the damned insignificant girls. With Édouard gone, there was no one else she trusted. She'd have to oversee everything now. She'd hunt down Kirill after she finished with the girls. And the scientists? She'd spared none of them. Not one had intervened to save Édouard, and he'd been worth a hundred of them. They'd watched on, doing nothing while Meiling sliced out his heart. There would always be more scientists eager to earn absurd amounts of money for easy work.

She'd lingered longer drawing out the life force of every one of her vampire minions. They *really* could have done something—anything—to save Édouard. Yes, they hadn't been in the lab with him at the time, but they had preternatural hearing and speed, for fuck's sake! Instead, they'd scratched their pretty asses and later begged her to spare them. She snorted her disgust aloud. Good riddance. They did nothing to protect her from the only true threat to her existence.

There was no one left on her side now, no one to keep her informed of any developments in the super-natural community, to warn her if discovery of her one all-important secret might be imminent. Once more, she was fully alone in the world, a warrior with her own cause, fighting, always fighting to endure.

The other immortals who shared this planet with her weren't nearly as mindful to conceal their existence, and they, too, were singling out the strongest wolf shifters and werewolves. She'd long suspected their deployment of hunters was their version of natural selection. And Cyrus with his pit-fighting pounds? His ego had always been too big for his britches. He was drawing too much attention to all of them. Unkillable as he was, his actions alone would inspire someone to search for the way to end him. And once someone figured out how to kill him, or another one of them, they'd know how to end her too.

Cassia scented a hare and immediately pivoted to chase it down. Her muscles obeying her every command, she tore through the underbrush, branches and trees whipping by her.

That first bite into warm flesh was ecstatic. Blood flowed down her chin while her eyes rolled upward. Had she been in her human form with hands to hold her prize, she'd have licked her lips. Instead, she chomped into the hare, ripping flesh from bone, crunching, savoring, tasting its fear. When she began picturing her catch as Meiling, she relished her capture even more.

Her meal was over too soon, so she continued the hunt. Meiling's scent was all over the forest, and it didn't take someone as brilliant as her to deduce where the girl was headed. So predictable. The kill would almost be too easy. Meiling was headed to Naya's pack; two of the sisters would be there for her at once. If only the journey to Lara were shorter, Cassia would retrieve her before heading to Colorado. But Cassia was close now, and her patience was all gone. She craved the relief of exacting punishment.

Unconcerned with borders or the rules of men, she ran through one mountainous forest after another, taking no preventions to avoid hunters. Not the kind that pursued wolf shifters, but the mundane kind, wholly unaware of an entire supernatural world right beneath their ignorant noses. She welcomed the chance to take one of them down, to vent her frustration on any of them. But though she crossed in and out of hunting zones, no one aimed at her.

Her drive to reach Meiling and Naya built. Her determination egged her on even when she tired.

She ran and ran across vast open spaces, unin-habited by man, recalling what it had been like to live before the planet swarmed with people, like an ant infestation—until after several days she finally dropped from exhaustion. Her travels were exactly as incredible as she'd imagined. She'd never felt wilder, freer, or more alive. Finally, her immortality meant something visceral, real, and tangible. The elongation of her muscles felt like a miracle, her every breath a gift. When the wind rippled across her fur, the sensations nearly overwhelmed her. Stalking her next meal was the most invigorating game she'd ever played, and when she got to tear into her kill, it was as if she were absorbing the animal's life force as she did via her kiss of death.

Killing to survive had never made her feel more alive.

She turned her full attention to her next target.

Meiling and Naya. Then Lara.

She'd had a small eternity to hone her skills as a predator. She'd lay a trap for them—simply because she could—and she'd revel in watching them fall into it.

Right before she gobbled them up...

CHAPTER NINE

NAYA

DAYS HAD PASSED since Mav announced they were going to war—and they hadn't gone anywhere.

The Moonlit Mountains compound was packed with shifters, all of them on edge. Even the children were restless, and they were protected from the worst of the situation, insulated from the latest news.

Maverick had put out a rallying call that brought Boone, beta of the Northwestern Pack, and Zasha and Quannah of the Smoky Mountain Pack. The three of them had arrived the day before.

The wizard brothers, along with their assistant Fianna, disappeared for a while, but the brothers had returned, this time with a small, talkative owl named Sir Lancelot instead of the fairy.

It was he that about sixty wolves were gathered in the Huddle listening to at present.

Naya, who sat sandwiched between Bruno and Clove, with Meiling on Bruno's other side in the first row beneath the platform where Maverick sat, couldn't help but notice how quickly things had changed. Last time, when Maverick had been alerted of danger, he hadn't wanted her to leave his side, positioning her up on the dais where she was within easy reach.

Granted, he could jump down the single step that separated the stage from the audience and reach her in nearly the same amount of time, but still ... the difference in seating arrangement was noteworthy. It didn't matter that Mav might have a slew of reasons for changing things up. For one, she now had a mate who was as strong as he was and wouldn't leave her side, and when he did it was never for long. But more so, Naya feared, it was the loud, ginormous elephant in the room that no one much mentioned but she couldn't stop thinking about: After a lifetime of believing herself the savior of werewolfkind, she was no more special than any other werewolf now.

Her entire life she'd rebelled against the implications of being said savior. She'd lashed out against her invisible prison, her blatant limitations, and everything she had to give up to fulfill her duty. Her responsibility.

Her fate.

And it'd all been nonsense. A fabrication.

A wicked and vicious manipulation by a terrible mind.

Naya knew full well seething wouldn't do her any good, and yet seethe she did. All day. All night. Except for those moments of relief—and undeniable bliss—when Bruno distracted her, pulling her away from the weight of the many deceptions and disappointments. Bruno was quite skilled at distracting her until her mind felt it was about to melt and no thoughts remained beyond gratitude for the connection he and she shared.

But damn Cassia.

Fuck. Her.

How many lives had she destroyed with her greed and selfishness? Because, apparently, eternal life wasn't enough for the woman—the monster.

Clove leaned her head next to Naya's shoulder and whispered, "He's just so fucking cute, isn't he?"

Naya blinked as she returned to the present. Her brow furrowed as she scanned the many shifters surrounding them. She saw a whole lot of strong, fierce, and sexy shifters, but no one who was ... cute. Unless she was talking about ... maybe Jasper?

Clove rolled her eyes. "The owl. The fucking owl, Ni." She nibbled on one side of her mouth as she considered. "Seems a bit wrong to say 'fucking' when

I'm talking about the owl, doesn't it? He's just so …
polite. And smart." She scrunched her nose. "Weird.
I really thought 'fuck' could apply to any life situation. But I guess not. Hunh."

At least Clove was still Clove. Despite all the
upheaval in Naya's life, Clove remained a reliable
constant.

Naya tuned into the—undeniably cute—pygmy
owl who stood on a table in front of Mav, River, and
Blake, staring out at his audience with enormous, all-
seeing eyes.

"I was a young pip of an owlet then," he was
saying in a clear voice that rang louder than his six-
inch height would suggest possible. "I wasn't yet
capable of absorbing the full implications of the fact,
but I do remember hearing that an immortal woman
had killed her immortal father. At the time, the information was only whispered about by intimidated
mages in dark corners, who didn't pay much mind to
an unobtrusive owl kept as a pet or a curiosity.
Immortals were a new invention of the time, and no
one yet knew what power they might possess to allow
them to manipulate the effects of time to such an
extent to grant themselves immortality."

"Wait," Naya said softly to Clove. "Did he just …
is he saying he's been alive as long as Cassia has?"

Clove stared at her, the scowl she gave her equal

parts amusement and concern. "Girl, where the fuck've you been? He just explained that like two minutes ago."

"So ... yes? He's been around as long as Cassia?"

Clove's mouth dropped the mirth and settled into full-on worry. "Yeah, plus, he has a photographic memory. Can you imagine that shit? He's been around for more than a thousand fucking years *and* he's never forgotten a damn thing about any of it."

"Sounds ... potentially unpleasant."

Clove shrugged, then shushed her, something Naya didn't think her loquacious, loudmouth friend had ever done before.

Sir Lancelot was saying, "For as important as the existence of immortal beings was, and for how recent our discovery of them was at the time, it's noteworthy that any mention of the woman and her father disappeared from history. I've been unable to find a single reference to the father in any resource, beyond my memory."

He paused to look out at his audience with a *And I should have been able to find something* upturn of the fluffy feathers surrounding his beak.

Albacus, who hovered in the air off to the side of the long conference table next to his brother, added, "You're saying you think Cassia suppressed the information."

"Of course," Sir Lancelot said in a squeaky voice that still managed to carry authority. "If not, it would be a fact that certainly someone would have recorded. The birth of immortals shouldn't be forgotten."

"And the fact that it was," Mordecai chimed in, "suggests that either Cassia has the kind of magic capable of controlling a situation such as this one, or she worked with a mage to do it."

Sir Lancelot spun around on his taloned feet to nod at the brothers. "Precisely."

The owl overlapped his wings behind his back as if he were clasping them together and began pacing the length of the desk. "She's clearly quite capable of orchestrating events to her benefit. What she's done with the young women, breeding them just for her experiments ... that suggests a highly rational and patient mind."

Naya squirmed and glanced across Bruno to share a look with Meiling. They'd had the chance to catch up and answer each other's questions, but she was the only one there who truly understood how Naya felt. They needed to talk again, no matter that she now looked like the woman Naya most despised in the entire world.

For as much as Bruno already seemed to know her better than was logical, he hadn't been lied to his entire life. He hadn't built his very existence around a fallacious construct.

As if he felt her unease, Bruno rested his hand on her thigh and squeezed. Naya allowed his comfort to soothe her ragged heart. The previous days had been too tumultuous and too exhausting to turn down any soothing.

Naya leaned back in her seat and placed her hand atop Bruno's, marveling at how strong, firm, and very much real it was. There he was: her mate. She'd never allowed herself to even dream of him, and yet *voilà*, here he was.

Sir Lancelot ceased his pacing to stare forward again, whisking his intent gaze across all of them in one big sweep before saying, "I think it's safe to assume that if Cassia so successfully erased all evidence of dispatching her father, another immortal, and that neither I nor Lords Albacus or Mordecai of Irele have been able to find a hint of how to end her eternal existence, it won't be easy. Furthermore, if she's proven herself this deceptive and calculating, I think it's likely she's expecting us to come after her in an attempt to eliminate her."

Mav frowned, his arms crossed tightly across his chest. "What are you saying, that we shouldn't even bother going after her?"

A general grumble of discontent swept through the crowd.

The little owl, unblinking, gazed at Mav for a few beats. "Not at all, Alpha. What I was eventually going to say is that Cassia will be prepared for your assault. Everything the woman does suggests her every move is considered and planned. And unless you are equipped with a surefire method to kill her, the immortal will fight you, likely hurt you and your pack, and survive to keep doing it as many times as you attack her."

The pygmy owl swept his wings in front of him, spun until he pinned Naya and Meiling in his stare, then pointed feathered wingtips at both of them. "You have, however, a potential solution right here."

Mav growled, which caused River and Blake to growl too.

Sir Lancelot ruffled his feathers but didn't otherwise flinch. "I agreed to the Lords of Irele transporting me here not to give you advice, but information. I understand full well that you are perfectly capable of receiving your own counsel. But as a creature who has known the two brothers of Irele for most of their lives, I will tell you this: if they think this is the only way to truly end Cassia, and from what you've told me this is a priority for you and your pack, then I would believe them. There are no finer or more informed wizards in the entire supernatural community than they. They are, without exaggeration, the best at what they do."

Sir Lancelot paused with another glance at Meiling and then Naya, which made both Bruno and Clove growl. "If the two sisters can combine their energy so that they both have immortality magic, then they have a chance to draw away Cassia's own immortality."

After that, the owl was silent while many shifters studied Naya and Meiling. Now that the two of them were no longer the saviors of a species, their secrets were shared with the entire pack. Everyone knew that Naya wasn't whom they'd believed her to be all her life.

Sir Lancelot asked Maverick, "Alpha, are there any more questions you'd like to ask of me about my knowledge of the history of the magical world before I depart?"

"No," Mav said. "You've illuminated us enough. Thank you for coming."

Naya couldn't decide if Maverick was being sarcastic or not. The alpha who'd been like a father to her seemed as conflicted as she was by recent developments. His eyes were shadowed, the draw of his mouth constantly tense and wary.

Sir Lancelot tipped his head in a formal bow.

"Then it's been my great pleasure, Maverick Dune, Alpha of the Rocky Mountain Pack. I lament only that I had no better news to deliver, or more helpful suggestions."

The owl faced the audience, bowed again. "I bid you all farewell. And I wish you speed, agility, and a great deal of good fortune, that you may end the woman who's proven so unworthy of the incredible gift she's been given."

The Rocky Mountain Pack wolves, who were more gruff and wild than polite, lobbed back a few *thank-yous* and *farewells*. Naya couldn't help but smile at the departing owl, who flew straight into a sparking web of light that opened between the two wizard brothers. In a flash of multi-colored lights, the owl was swallowed whole.

While Naya had been studying the owl and wizards, Maverick had been studying her. When a hush settled across the room again, he asked Albacus and Mordecai, "What are the odds that your plan will work?"

"Which part?" Albacus asked.

"The part where we merge the girls' energy?" Mordecai asked. "Or the part where they pull the immortality magic out of the thousand-plus-year-old immortal?"

Maverick glared at them. "Both."

"Ah," Albacus said and *ah-he-hemmed*.

"Well..." Mordecai said. "Neither is guaranteed to work, but both appear to be our best options at the moment."

"Right," Albacus said. "We merge the energy of the girls, and if that's successful—"

"If?" Maverick said, his nostrils flaring and the skin along his exposed forearms rippling. His wolf was a moment away from popping free.

Mordecai shrugged. "Yes, if. We won't make promises we can't keep. *If* it works—"

"And it likely will," Albacus said with a placating smile.

"Then it's the best chance any of us have at ending the threat that Cassia poses to the entire supernatural community."

Mav's lips pressed into a line so hard that his lips lightened from their usual pink. "The risk is too steep."

Not when I no longer hold the ability to save werewolves from extinction.

Albacus shrugged. "The alternative is just to let Cassia be. Maybe she won't cause any more trouble. Perhaps she's finished with her ambitions that injure others."

Not a single person sitting in that room believed that.

"Can you transfer the immortality magic from Meiling to someone else?" Zasha of the Smoky Mountain Pack asked. "I'd like to show Cassia what I think of her playing puppet master with people's lives."

"No," Quannah said next to her before he was interrupted by a melody of chimes.

The wizard brothers were shaking their heads, small ceramic beads knocking into each other despite the mages' half-solid nature.

"We can only do it with the twins," Mordecai said.

"Since their energy signature is so similar as to be almost identical," Albacus added. "We'll be lucky to transfer it between Meiling and Naya, but no one else."

Zasha's mate Quannah didn't bother to hide his relief. The man wore his expressions openly on his normally stoic face. The relief in his dark eyes said he'd jump through fire a million times before accepting that Zasha might put herself in the line of danger.

Was that what Bruno looked like when he considered her? She glanced at him.

His beautiful lips were pressed into a scowl. His usually bright, dancing eyes were set with determined conviction.

When he noticed her attention on him, he met her eyes. "You can't do it, *peligrosa*," he said. "You can't."

Only she could.

And she would.

She had to.

There was no other way. Hadn't he been listening?

She squeezed his hand in empty reassurance, then leaned forward to look at Meiling.

Her borrowed violet eyes said exactly what Naya was thinking: *Let's do it, and let's do it soon. We gotta kill a bitch.*

CHAPTER TEN

BRUNO

THE MATTRESS SHIFTED BESIDE HIM, and Bruno stretched his hand to trail against Naya's bare back as she sat up. His fingers alighted along her warm skin, as soft as a dream, while, gingerly, he traced the length of the fresh scar that sliced across her ribcage.

Not that long ago, he'd almost lost her. She'd died before they'd had the chance to consummate their bond, but he'd brought her back to life.

They'd gotten another chance.

A chance he had no desire to squander.

"Training again?" he asked, his question soft in the descending night. Though the curtains were drawn along the windows of her cabin, he knew it must be around twilight. When she slept at his side, he rarely did, unable to shut off his thoughts, always searching for another way, a different solution to the threat that was Cassia, one that didn't endanger Naya.

"Yeah." Naya glanced over her shoulder at him. "Gotta work some stuff out. No better way than a punching bag."

His woman was both hard and soft at once. Determined and fierce, and yet she opened up to him like a blooming flower, revealing to him her inner petals, the most tender buds. When they made love, her vulnerability shone through her eyes. Now, he saw none of that vulnerability. The weight of bringing down the immortal tensed her shoulders and her abdomen, accentuating the ridges of her muscles.

"It's not all on you to deal with Cassia," he said, working not to let it sound like the plea it was when he wanted to shout to the heavens that he needed her to stay with him, to beg her never to leave his side. To tell her how, though they'd met less than three months before, it would break him to lose her. Brother Wolf would never choose another. It was her or nothing. Her or devastation.

Like a languorous cat, she leaned into his touch for a few moments, then rose from the bed, and opened her closet to pull out a fresh set of exercise clothing.

"It pretty much is all on me though, isn't it? Me and Mei." She spoke facing her closet when she already clutched her chosen shorts and bra top. She'd been doing it often, avoiding looking at him when discussing the risk she was going to take. And by now he was convinced she was going to do it, no matter what he said. No matter what he did. She was going to agree to the wizards' plan.

Bruno tossed off the sheet that had tangled across his legs and walked over to her, looping his hands around her waist, enjoying the feel of her naked body pressed against his, that familiarity that could only exist between true mates.

"You have *me*. You have Mav and the rest of your pack, including crazy Clove. You have the mages, and Zasha, Quannah, and the support of their pack. Even Boone is willing to ally with us."

She turned in his hold, leaning her face back so she could peer up into his. The sadness in her smile made his heart squeeze. For the previous three days, since the wizard brothers announced their perilous plan, he'd been trying so hard not to reveal how afraid he really was.

But, after Cassia's web of lies had imprisoned Naya for her entire life, he couldn't now be the one to ask her not to do what she thought was right. As important as it was for her to remain with him, he refused to clip her wings. He wouldn't ask her to be anything other than the fierce warrior that she was.

However, if Maverick were to command her not to merge energy signatures with Meiling ... now that was a course of action Bruno could readily get behind.

Naya ran the back of a hand along his cheek. "You know that if there was another way—any other way—I'd be the first one in line to vote for that."

Though it was dim in the room, his preternatural sight could easily make out the intensity of her blue eyes. They said, *I want what you want too.*

Then stay, he responded, pushing his desire through his own eyes. *Give us the chance we deserve.*

After staring at him for a few more moments, she pressed her lips to his in a feather-light kiss. Once more his heart panged; that felt too much like a memory, like the ghost of a kiss—as if she were already leaving him, or worse, already gone.

Instinctively, he drew her closer, pressing their bodies together, her curves complementing the angles of his body as if each had been designed for the other.

She withdrew her mouth from his and offered him a regretful smile. "You know I can't stand by and let Cassia keep doing what she does, not when there's a chance Mei and I can stop her."

Bruno didn't say anything. It was a conversation they'd been having for the last three days, and it always came back around to the same point. Naya was the kind of person who couldn't do nothing when she had an opportunity to spare the world from the suffering and devastation Cassia wrought wherever she went.

He had nothing left to say that he hadn't already voiced. He tried instead to fill any openings in their days and nights with passionate, wild love-making, with gentle caresses and kisses that lingered across the skin, with the kind of abandon of two people who understood their days together might very well be numbered, all the loving and connection and excitement they might share over the long lifetimes of shifters.

"I haven't yet had my fill of you," he whispered, his breath hot against her neck. She shivered and tilted her head out of the way to allow him better access.

"I should hope not," she said, but her voice was already husky, thickening with desire. For two people who'd never had sex before meeting each other, they'd done a fine job of making up for lost time.

Sweeping kisses, each hotter than the last, across the line of her neck, he said, "I need centuries to get through the list of things I want to do with you." He kissed her collarbone. "To you." He chuckled, the heat of his breath igniting the point above her breasts. "I also have a long list of things I want you to do to me."

She half-grunted, half-moaned, arching her back and pressing her bare breasts forward. "I'd ask about the list," she muttered, "but I don't want to think anymore."

"Hmmm." His lips vibrated against the swell of one breast. "Is that so?"

"Yeah. Thinking's so fucking overrated. I'm so over it, you have no idea."

"Tell me more." But he didn't really mean it. He trailed his tongue around one nipple before pulling it into his mouth and sucking hard.

Her breath caught and her head fell back with the kind of wanton moan that made his dick pulse with need.

He dragged his mouth to the other breast, his lips gliding along the hot skin between them, while running the pad of a thumb across the slick surface of the first nipple. When he drew the nipple of the second breast into his mouth, his tongue hot and wet, he pinched the other one.

She gasped and flung the clothes she'd still been holding in one hand behind them with abandon.

They thumped dully against the wall, then slid to the floor.

When he flicked his tongue across the hardened nipple, she sucked in a breath so ragged that a wave of desire shot through him, from head to toe, pulsing in his groin.

As his free hand slid down her body, trailing across her flat stomach until it slipped between her slick folds, she groaned loudly enough that Maverick would certainly hear her if he was in his cabin next door.

Bruno didn't care anymore. Clearly Naya didn't either.

He slipped a finger inside her, and this time, when she groaned, he did too.

"Oh my ... holy ... *fuck!*" she panted, then tightened the wall around his finger. The hot tunnel was the path to oblivion, to losing his mind and loving every second of it.

Without warning, she grabbed his hand, pulled it out of her, and yanked it away. He only had a moment for his brow to crease in confusion before she wrapped her arms around his neck and jumped, winding her legs around his waist.

He growled and turned around, walking them toward the bed, and though it was only on the other side of the small room, before they'd reached it Naya squeezed her legs around his hips, lifted up, and slid down—purposefully slowly, torturously—onto the length of him with a long, deep, extended, *groan.* Her eyes rolled up into her head as she flung it back, her long hair tickling his thighs. His knees buckled and he moaned salaciously, almost coming undone right there.

"*Peligrosa,* you're my undoing," he growled and dug his strong fingers into the delectable curve of her ass, squeezing hard enough to make her gasp, then giggle.

Lowering her to the bed, he held her hips tilted up against his while he admired the body he got to worship. She was perfection, even her angry-looking scar. She was a survivor, a fighter. *His.*

Mate.

Before he was finished studying her, she yanked him down on top of her, and when his torso pressed up against hers, her breasts hot and tantalizing against him, he couldn't remain still any longer. He drove into her with the fervent need to prove that she belonged right where she was. That the force of his will alone could keep her there with him.

Her hips rose to meet each one of his thrusts. She raked her nails along his back before gripping his ass and tugging him against her.

Harder.

Faster.

Deeper.

Her hands guided his pelvis to smack against hers.

More, more, more.

He gave her what she wanted, what she demanded.

What *he* needed—until their bodies were slick with sweat, their minds blank, and their hearts full.

He'd led her to climax again and again, immersing himself in the squeaking and gasping and hitching sounds of her nearly unbearable pleasure, of the way she squeezed her eyes shut and alternately bit her lip or opened her mouth in the face of overwhelming sensation. The way whenever she was close to cresting into oblivion, she clutched him harder, pulled him closer, wanting to take him there with her.

Wherever she went, she wanted him at her side.

He'd follow her anywhere.

When she finally collapsed on top of him in a tangle of limp, sweaty limbs, he folded her into his arms like a precious treasure, and she pressed her face against his chest, where she could hear the rapid thumping of his heart.

He breathed in the scent of her as he draped a leg

across hers. Mint shampoo and lavender soap, sweat and sex. Like his perfect mate.

He kissed the crown of her head before attempting to memorize what this moment felt like, just in case.

Once her breathing evened out, he ran fingers along the length of her hair. "Ready for a shower?"

"Mmmm."

"I know you. You won't want to fall asleep all sweaty."

"Mmmm. Mmm-hmm."

"Come on, *amor*. I'll do all the soaping up. All you have to do is stand there and look beautiful."

"Oh yeah?" Her voice was still groggy, but suddenly more alert.

"*Sí*. I'll do all the work. Whatever you want..."

"Tempting offer," she mumbled.

"I aim to tempt," he growled softly. "And to please."

"Well, then consider yourself successful on both counts."

He sat up, sliding her across his body as he went, preparing to help her into the shower. If she was this relaxed, she should sleep. She'd been resting more than him, but it still wasn't enough. She'd need all her strength to confront the immortal.

"Mmm, not yet," she mumbled. "I just want to lie here with you a bit more first."

In that moment, all they were was mates. Lovers. There were no destinies or burdens, only the burgeoning love between them.

"*Te amo*," he murmured into her hair.

"Mm-hmm, I love you too."

Then, slicked with sweat, Naya fell asleep in his arms. For the first time in three days, he knew complete peace.

He allowed his eyes to drift shut too, slumping back down in the bed with her.

Their shared peace was guaranteed to end far too soon...

CHAPTER ELEVEN

BRUNO

TWO MORE NIGHTS PASSED, but Bruno was no closer to accepting the decision it seemed inevitable Naya would make. He wasn't the only one. He'd overheard more than one conversation where the parties lamented the dangers Naya would be exposing herself to. There were no guarantees the wizards' spell would work or, if it did, that Naya and Meiling would survive their encounter with Cassia. Naya might no longer be their savior, but she was still one of their own.

All of Rocky Mountain Pack, even the children, were on edge, in a constant state of readiness, all jumpy, twitchy, and prone to snarling or snapping at each other at the slightest provocation—him included.

Bruno couldn't get his shoulders to stop creeping

up toward his neck. The stress burdening them all was palpable. Though it was nearly 3 a.m., the expansive training complex was bustling. With Maverick calling the wolves from their satellite locations to the Moonlit Mountains location, the gym was full at all hours. Even their visiting allies came there to work off the extra energy—and to remain sharp.

Their enemy was out there, possibly stronger than ever now that Cassia had incorporated the magic of a wolf shifter.

Clove leaned into Bruno, speaking up at him since she was so much shorter. "Wow, huh? It's kinda *hawt* to watch them, am I right?"

Bruno rolled his eyes, mostly out of a now-habitual response to Naya's mouthy friend. He'd given up trying to shake her, focusing instead on her loyalty to his mate to minimize his irritation at her constant presence. The small woman was clearly upset at the prospect of Naya taking down Cassia with no one to help her but her twin sister.

Who no longer looked anything like her...

Bruno was watching the same spectacle Clove was. It was hard for anyone to resist the intensity with which Naya and Meiling fought each other, and for him it was all but impossible.

A small crowd had gathered around the mat off

in one corner of the gym. At first, the spectators had been more or less quiet, but after the first ten minutes they'd begun cheering the fighters on. The sisters had been at it for nearly an hour now, and the volume of the crowd rivaled that of a public boxing match.

"Fuck yeah, Ni!" a woman yelled when Naya landed a kick to Meiling's ribcage with a satisfying smack.

"Ow," a few of them whined when Meiling retaliated, nailing a sophisticated combination kick-jab strike.

Back and forth they went, equally matched despite their differing training. Their stamina was as admirable as their combat skills. Though both women were breathing heavily, neither was drooping. Even in a pack of wolf shifters with advanced strength and healing, Bruno guessed most of them would have called the match by then.

But not Naya, not his woman. She gave the impression that nothing would stop her. Ever.

He hoped with a feverish desperation that would turn out to be the case.

Clove elbowed him in the waist. "Come on, admit it. Watching them go at it is turning you on."

The truth was that just about anything Naya did revved his engine. The more he got of her, the more he craved her. Over the years, he'd heard this was the case with mates. But he hadn't anticipated that he'd yearn for her the very moment she stepped away from him. Even when she was in his arms, he wanted to record every sensation, to expand on the feeling of her.

Clove *pffted* at his side. "Don't ignore me, Bruno. It's fucking rude."

He couldn't help but snort at the irony of her statement. She was the rudest person he'd ever met.

"It's weird as fuck to see Meiling in the creepy immortal's body, no doubt," Clove continued, undeterred. "But, damn, Cassia was a fine-ass woman."

That was true, but no one could be as beautiful to him as his mate. Though he was watching the two women move around the mat, the only time he studied Meiling was to anticipate how she'd strike his mate, how she'd defend against Naya.

When Clove huffed at his side, he finally said, "It's fascinating to watch them spar like this. Their moves are different, and yet strikingly similar in their elegance."

"Fuck yeah, my girl's moves are elegant. Meiling must train like a mofo to be able to match Ni when she's in the ring. And lucky for her the immortal bitch wasn't some lard-ass couch potato, or no way would she be able to get her new body to move like that."

"I've never seen some of Mei's moves before."

"Well, that makes sense though, right? Not many people lining up to study under a bunch of blood-sucking assholes."

Only, Bruno wondered if there might be. Vampires were master manipulators, and ones as old and powerful as those who ran the Shèng Shān Monastery were bound to be better at it than most.

He said, "Mei's been training all her life, and very hard from how she tells the story. Although, as you say, there must be some adjustment for Mei to a new body unused to training as hard as she did."

"So, like Ni. Good. And look at Mei move! No doubt she'll get used to being in Cassia real fast. Chick is fluid, man, which is fucking amazing. They're gonna need every advantage they can get to take the bitch out."

For the first time, Bruno thought he glimpsed through Clove's bravado.

He hesitated, but then admitted, "I don't want her to go. I don't care what Cassia might do to others, I don't want her to have the chance to do any of it to Naya."

Clove swirled to face him even as Meiling swept a leg beneath Naya as his mate landed from a jumping kick. Naya managed to skirt out of the way, just in time.

"Ohmyholyfuck, Bruno," Clove was saying. "I can't fucking stand the idea of my girl going out to face Cassia all alone. I mean, sure, she's got a badass vamp-fu fighter at her side, but that's not enough. It's nowhere near enough." Clove was rushing all her words together as if they'd been bottled up, desperate to break free: "Cassia is an immortal. A fucking *immortal* who can do all sorts of scary shit. Ni told me Cassia actually exploded a vamp. Blew him the fuck up. And that was a master vamp. And she can fly. I mean, what the hell're Ni and Mei supposed to do about a crazy-ass bitch who has no heart and can fucking *fly*?"

Bruno's cheek twitched; he didn't think that had ever happened before. He trained his focus on Naya and Mei as they danced around the ring, so equal in skill that they had to work harder to find an opening for a strike that might actually make a difference.

For a few moments, he pretended Clove's concerns didn't pierce him straight in the heart.

Then he spun on her, jaw clenched tightly, until he whisper-shouted at her, "Don't you think I know all that? I can't sleep or eat, and whenever I manage to do either it's only because I'm forcing myself to so I can be strong for her. *Mierda*, Clove. I know, I know, *I know* all that. I've been all but begging her not to do it."

Clove, unperturbed by his agitation, nodded encouragement. "Great, that's great. Keep that shit up. And what's she say when you tell her you don't want her to do it?"

"What do you think?" Brother Wolf was snarling inside him, unused to feeling impotent. "She's going to do it anyway."

"Dude, you've gotta get down on your knees and really beg her. Make her see reason."

He smiled sadly at her before turning his gaze back to the mat in front of them. The shifters around them were cheering. Whatever they were celebrating, he'd missed it.

"I can't beg her to stay," he said so softly that if Clove hadn't been a wolf shifter, she would have missed it over the boisterous ruckus that had erupted around them.

The smack of flesh hitting flesh pierced the din, but he closed his eyes anyway. "Naya has been trapped here her entire life. She's been a prisoner."

"Yeah, of Cassia's invention. Not really."

"But she didn't know that. She's told me how she could never go anywhere. How she wanted to see the world and she hasn't been able to leave her pack's territory. How that tormented her."

For once, Clove was quiet.

"She's been told what to do all her life. Every

day, her decisions have been about what's best for all werewolves, not her. Every decision, everything she's done has been for someone else."

"If you're suggesting that going after Cassia is for her, then you're dead wrong."

He opened his eyes. "I'm not. I know she wants to do it to save others from whatever Cassia will do over the rest of however long she might live."

"Basically forever," Clove said. "It's fucked up. Why would she be given all this power and immortality when she sucks at it?"

To that, Bruno had no answer. So he said, "I can't be the one now to tell her what to do, to keep her from doing what she thinks she should."

Clove stepped in front of him, giving her back to the fight. With effort, Bruno dragged his gaze from the graceful efficient movements of Naya's body, slick with sweat, down to her friend, whose expression was filled with more ferocious intent then he'd ever seen on her before.

"If you're about to spout some bullshit nonsense about how you can't be the one to lock her in her gilded fucking cage, save it, buster. If you don't do whatever you can to keep her here, she's gonna face down a fucking immortal who kills master vamps like it's her warmup. You get that, right? You understand what she'll be heading into?"

He scowled at her. "*Carajo*, of course I know. I'm the one who's seen what immortals are capable of firsthand. I understand the dangers fully."

"Then fuck your highhanded, lofty notions of what a mate should and shouldn't do. This isn't some twisted fairy tale where shit'll turn out right for the heroine just because she has a hero waiting for her back home."

He glared at her. "*I know.*"

"Then you'd better do something about it, mister. She won't listen to me, and believe me I've tried. She just gives me this lofty speech about how she's gotta do what's right, how she's always known she'd have to sacrifice her safety for the wellbeing of others, that she's been doing it always, it just looks a little different now, blah, blah, blah."

Clove stepped closer to him, tilting her head all the way up to nail him with a brutal stare. Her eyes flashed the gold of her pack's magic.

"You'd better use that dick of yours to convince her."

He blinked at her. "Excuse me?"

She waved a hand between them, tsking. "Don't give me that 'excuse me' shit. We all know what you've been up to when you're shacked up in Naya's cabin. I'm surprised Mav hasn't murdered you yet. Must be because of all the other pressing crazy that's happening, 'cause if not, trust me, you'd be dead as a doorknob."

She paused, softening by a fraction.

She sighed. "Look, she loves you, man. Like, for real. You're it for her. Mates till the end, the whole shebang. I need you to be a motherfucking snake charmer and get her to change her mind."

He arched his brows. "A snake charmer? Really?"

"Yes, really. Use that fine snake of yours to over-power her will. Make her see sense."

He didn't respond.

"And in case you're missing my point here, your snake's your *dick*."

"Yeah, I understood that."

"Good. Then use it. Work your magic. Make her lose her mind. Fuck her till she forgets Cassia's name, maybe even her own. She's surely earned it. Just ... take care of my girl for me."

The gold of her pack magic calmed, and her eyes glistened. "Make her stay, okay? I really need her to be all right." She sniffed, allowing Bruno to see clear through the tough veneer.

He scowled, but pulled her into a one-armed hug. "Come here." Her plan, at the very least, was the best plan he'd heard yet. But even that wouldn't work.

She wrapped her arms around his waist as he said, "You have no idea how much I want to carry out your plan. But I can't. You know I can't."

She looked up. "But you can! Of course you can."

He shook his head, allowing some of his sadness to show on his face. He smiled, his heart aching. "I'm her mate. I can't ask anything of her that will interfere with who she is. With who she wants to be."

"Not even if it's the only thing that'll keep her alive?"

"She's strong enough. So is Meiling. They'll have each other and all of us to back them up."

Clove pulled away from him, scowling. "More BS. I'd do anything to keep Naya safe."

"So will I."

"No, not the one thing that could actually change things."

"You forget that I've already asked. I did at the start. She knows how I feel. How could she not? I'm latching on to her like a tick whenever she gives me the chance. She *knows* how I feel, what I want. She knows I want to spend the rest of my life with her. But I can't ask her to be something she's not."

Clove scoffed. "You can't ask her to stay alive?"

"I can't ask her to be a coward. You know that's not who she is."

Clove opened her mouth, closed it, frowned, and

turned around to watch the rest of the fight. He leaned down to tell her, "If Naya were in danger, you and I would run through fire to get her back safely."

"Of course we motherfucking would."

"Well, she just wants to do the same for us."

"But we're not in danger."

"Oh, but we are. Every supernatural and human alive is so long as she's out there."

Clove hmmped while Bruno shook his head, muttering under his breath at himself.

"*La puta mierda.*" If he hadn't just made Naya's argument for her...

Discordant applause, along with whistles, hoots, and hollers, interrupted the heavy direction of his thoughts. The fight was over.

You all right? Naya asked him across their mate link.

He discovered her staring at him, singling him out of the crowd.

He forced a smile, which was unlikely to convince her, but it was the best he could do at the moment. *I'm fine. Great fight, amor.*

Mei's amazing, isn't she?

Not as amazing as you are, peligrosa.

Then Meiling stepped in front of Naya, half hugging her while they spoke. Though Meiling now had black hair to Naya's blond, and violet eyes to her blue, and a hundred other differences, Bruno could still tell the women were twin sisters. He couldn't be certain it wasn't because he already knew they were, but there was just something about the way they moved, their energy, that felt alike.

As the women stepped off the mat, Zasha, the alpha of the Smoky Mountain Pack, handed them towels, grinning at them, speaking loudly enough that Bruno could easily discern her voice from the rest.

"Damn, ladies," Zasha said. "Those were some fine fucking moves you had there."

Zasha was dressed in similar fashion to Naya and Mei, all three of them in stretchy shorts, sports tops that revealed tight abdomens, and long hair swept up into a high ponytail.

"Once you two've rested," Zasha said, "I'm up for another go." Zasha had sparred with Naya the day before, and Meiling the day before that. Between the three women, they could start their own school of female badassery.

"You up for it?" Zasha asked, while Naya and Meiling wiped up their sweat.

"Definitely," Naya said first.

"Of course," Meiling said after.

Zasha grinned and walked with them out into the milling shifters, who were patting them on the back and giving Naya fist-bumps, something new to Bruno.

"Awesome," Zasha said. "I haven't had this much fun in a ring in a long while."

Then Quannah caught her eye and she smiled at him. It was the kind of private smile Bruno had seen many times before, shared between mates.

"All right. Find me," she said and walked over to Quannah, who pulled her possessively against his side.

It was what Bruno wanted to do too. He moved toward Naya, but just as he was about to reach her, a pop pinged somewhere near him, hurting his ears. He winced and turned, spotting a fairy much like Fianna, except this one was clothed entirely in blue, with matching hair. She hovered above them all, speaking. When she wasn't heard, she brought a finger to each side of her mouth and whistled, loudly enough to make him grimace and pull away all over again.

Sudden silence blanketed the high-ceilinged warehouse-like building. Shifters pointed attentive stares up at the hummingbird-sized woman, whose translucent wings fluttered so rapidly that they were a blur behind her.

"The great wizards Mordecai and Albacus have arrived and request the presence of Naya of the

Rocky Mountain Pack and Meiling of the Shèng Shān Monastery."

As one, the Rocky Mountain Pack wolves, including Naya, directed their attention to their alpha, who stood off to the side, where he'd been speaking with his beta, gamma, and another two wolves Bruno didn't know by name.

Maverick looked from the fairy to Naya and back again. "Where are they?" he asked the diminutive messenger.

"Waiting in what they said was called the Huddle."

"Then, everyone, go there. I'll be there as soon as I have a word with Naya."

The shifters, including those who didn't take orders from the alpha, like Zasha, Quannah, and Boone, headed toward the multiple exits along the outer walls of the building. Those on other equipment, in the middle of their own workouts, dropped everything to hustle to obey Maverick's command.

Clove hesitated, obviously wanting to wait for Naya, but ultimately she left too.

But not Bruno.

He wasn't losing sight of Naya, not for a minute. Not when Cassia was still after her.

Meiling walked to join him, while Naya moved to speak with Maverick.

All Bruno could think was, *Dear God, please let him command her not to go through with the energy merging that would share Meiling's borrowed immortality magic with her.*

If her alpha ordered her to stay, she'd have to.

Bruno wouldn't be the one to deny her wish, no matter how selfless, and he'd have his beloved.

Meiling drew next to him and whispered, "Don't bother hoping. Whatever he says to her won't work. She's already made up her mind."

Bruno didn't answer her. He was too busy hoping Meiling was somehow wrong.

CHAPTER TWELVE

BRUNO

ONCE NAYA and Meiling arrived at the Huddle, Albacus and Mordecai didn't delay in asking the two women if they had reached a decision. Now that the brothers had composed a definitive plan on how to merge the two sisters' energy fields, they were uncharacteristically eager to get started—no long-winded, convoluted back-and-forth arguments about this, that, or the other.

It figured. The one time Bruno wanted them to draw things out, they were steamrolling toward the inevitable.

Naya had refused to meet Bruno's piercing gaze as she'd announced to the entire Rocky Mountain Pack and their guests that she was going to do the merge. If there was a way for her to spare others from the suffering Cassia inflicted, she said it was her duty to do her part.

Cheers, applause, *hell-yeahs*, and *go-Naya*s rang out across the communal center. Bruno and Maverick remained tight-lipped. Clove openly scowled, narrowing her eyes at Naya as if she felt like knocking some sense into her, and would be doing so at the earliest opportunity.

Only there would be no chance to attempt to change Naya's mind.

Not anymore.

Not that it'd make a difference. There was nothing left for Bruno to say that he hadn't tried already.

Once Naya and Meiling had confirmed their willingness to take part in the mages' plan, the half-dead wizards had quickly ushered them outside, with the assistance of their small fairy assistant, this one named Nessa, who was nearly as persistent as the previous one, Fianna.

They stood outside in a wide clearing near the Huddle, between worn paths that surrounded them on all sides, leading out to the residential areas of the pack holdings. Naya and Meiling were deep in hushed conversation with the wizards, surrounded by hundreds of shifters, all straining to pick up on what they were saying, Bruno especially.

"We think we'll be able to separate your energy fields later," Albacus was telling the young women.

"But you aren't sure?" Naya asked.

Mordecai chuckled, and the sound was far from reassuring. "My dear child, we aren't certain of much. Didn't we make that clear already? We didn't keep anything from you. The decision was yours alone to make."

"We're heading into uncharted territory," Albacus added. "Over the centuries, mages have attempted something like this."

"But not *this*."

"No, nothing exactly like this," Albacus said. "The existence of immortals has hardly been discussed in the annals of magic, and even then—"

"Largely as a hypothetical," Mordecai inserted.

"If you can't separate our energy bodies later..." Meiling said, patting her thighs in what Bruno had noticed was a habitual behavior for her—looking for the reassurance of her blades strapped to her body, but those were lost somewhere in the dense brush at the bottom of Shèng Shān Mountain. "What will that mean for us? Will Naya and I be able to lead separate lives after this?"

The many shifters surrounding the huddled wizards and sisters seemed to lean forward imperceptibly as they all waited for the answer.

"If we can't separate you after we perform this spell intended to unite you," Albacus said.

"And also assuming you survive Cassia's retaliation when confronted by your attack," Mordecai said, eliciting a chorus of growls, snarls, and curses, which he either ignored or didn't notice.

"Yeah, assuming all that," Naya said, snark riding her words, making them sharp.

"Well, then..." Albacus said with a dreamy smile, proving the two brothers were barely of this world, or perhaps that they did an excellent job of living in their own. "If we separate you, life will continue for you as normal. If we can't, then you may or may not be able to lead a life apart from your sister. It all depends."

"On what?" Naya asked.

"On what actually happens once we perform the spell, of course."

"As we've mentioned—" Mordecai said.

"An abundance of times," Albacus interjected.

"When performing new spells, things don't always go to plan."

Naya and Meiling stared at the wizards—hard.

Delight reached Albacus' eyes. "Sometimes they go remarkably better than we'd hoped."

"Oh, *oui*, sometimes that is the case," Mordecai said. "Magic doesn't always do as we expect, even when it theoretically should. It has its own, hmmm..." He paused to scratch the beard across his cheeks. "Personality, shall we say?"

Albacus was nodding, to a chorus of chimes. "Like a child. Miraculous, wild, and ... surprising." He grinned.

Bruno, who stood next to Maverick out in the clearing, closest to Naya, leaned his head toward the alpha. "Tell me again why you refuse to order her not to do this."

There was, of course, no need to clarify who *her* was. As much as Bruno might like and appreciate Meiling, she wasn't his mate.

At first Maverick bristled, but then he sighed, a heavy, regretful exhale. "I want to order her not to do it, Bruno. I really do. But..." He shook his head. "Her entire life, she's lived with the weight of putting the needs of others before her own. She's always known that she had to give up her wants for the greater good." The large man cracked his neck to either side, the pops loud. "She's become everything I ever hoped she would be. A ferocious, strong, and highly capable fighter. A selfless and generous woman. She is the best of werewolves."

"And yet you'll allow her to risk all that for an experimental spell by..." Bruno paused, wondering what to say about the half-dead-half-alive translucent wizards. "Well, I don't even know what to say about the two of them, they're so odd."

"*So* odd," Maverick echoed.

"You'll allow Naya to risk herself? She might never be the same after this spell. You heard what they said the other day. Neither one of them can guarantee the spell won't backfire and cause some, eh, how to say? Unexpected results." Bruno faced the alpha. "Mav, it could be really bad. They're all but admitting that."

Mav breathed slowly again, his eyes heavy. He rubbed the bridge of his nose. "I know, man, don't you think I fucking know? I've talked to the mages in private and it's all fucking killing me."

Bruno froze. "When? Without me?" A threat rolled through his question even if he didn't mean it to. After all, he was also a leader of his own pack. He wasn't used to being excluded from important discussions.

Alpha power pulsed out of Maverick forcefully enough that the wolves immediately surrounding them took a step back, casting curious glances at the two.

"Remember your place," Mav snapped.

"That's the thing," Bruno responded. "I am. That's my mate we're talking about."

Maverick turned his entire body to face Bruno, so

Bruno did the same. River and Blake noticed, pulling their attention away from the ongoing discussion between the mages and the sisters to them, walking in their direction.

"You have no official claim to her," Mav said. "Not without my permission."

"That's not how it works, and you know it."

Mav growled, and the wolves around them responded, doing the same, backing their alpha.

Naya looked over at them, but Bruno was too busy facing down the prick who disputed the fact that Bruno's wolf knew what she was to them. Beyond a doubt.

With a snarl curling his lip, Bruno took half a step toward Maverick, narrowing the space between them. By the way the shifters around them reacted, he might as well have thrown down the gauntlet.

He opened his mouth, prepared to make Maverick see how important it was to save Naya, that she was *his*. His mate. His future. His everything.

But then he paused and breathed. He called on the skills he'd honed over the years of being beta to his own pack and took the half step back.

"Look, Mav." Bruno rubbed his hands over his face. "I'm just freaked out, okay? I can't lose her. And the threats to her are just too great right now. This spell is only the start of it. She might not come back from it the same way she is now. What if it, *no sé*, what if it messes her up somehow? What if the mages merge her with Mei, but not their wolves? Naya could be cut off from her wolf ... or something equally terrible."

Disconnecting shifters from their wolves was a favorite experiment of the hunters. Whenever they managed it, afterward the shifter unerringly took their own lives, one way or another. A shifter wasn't meant to live without their wolf, and when it happened it wasn't an existence worth having.

"I've thought of that," Mav said, his words suddenly soft. "The mages even mentioned it."

"Then we can't," Bruno snarled from the sudden urgency of convincing the one man with the power to intervene before it was too late. "We can't let her do it. We can't risk her. She's too important."

To him. And to the wolf.

A hand landed on his back. He recognized the weight of Naya's touch and the lines of her fingers. Her scent and her particular warmth. Everything about her silently sang out *mate*. And if all of that wasn't enough, Brother Wolf was howling a greeting that was half-celebration she was still there with them and half lament that she soon would be taking on the most terrible enemy their kind had ever seen.

Naya pressed her chest against his arm as she

inserted herself between her mate and her alpha. "I *can* take the risk," she said, firm and resolute, "and I will. I have to." This time, she pointed her eyes only at Bruno. "It isn't up to you."

Though her words were harsh and cutting, their tone was sorrowful, regretful, almost as if they were an apology.

She switched to their telepathic mate bond; it was the only way to have any true privacy when surrounded by so many with supernatural hearing.

I wish it didn't have to be this way. She stepped away from Maverick and into his arms.

He pulled her body flush against his, wishing he could keep her there and safe with nothing beyond his physical strength. Immediately after, he regretted even thinking it. He wouldn't cage her, though his fear would happily lock her up in a bedroom with him and never allow her to leave his side.

He wanted to tell her, *It doesn't have to be this way. You can choose to stay with me. Always with me.* But though his every thought screamed his pleas through his own mind, he tamped them down, kissing her instead.

Promise me you'll survive the merging, he told her through their link, his lips dancing with hers gently, languorously, as if they had all the time in the world, while the stares of dozens of shifters burned against them, urging them to hurry.

Kissing him back with the tenderness of dreams, she said, *I promise.* And he clamped her closer while they both knew there was no way she could promise that.

He drew back from her to stare into her eyes, the crystalline bright blue of a cloudless sky. A hundred thoughts and fears coalesced inside him all at once, until he was poised to pop. He blinked them away, forced himself to be the kind of man he'd always been—before he'd discovered his mate and panicked every time he contemplated a life without her.

Aware that she likely saw right through him, he tried to smile. *Te amo, peligrosa.* He swallowed, his Adam's apple bobbing. *Now go kick some ass.*

"Naya."

He and Naya turned to find Meiling standing beside them. "We have to do this now," she said. "Cassia's heading in our direction. I can feel her."

"Right," Naya said. "I'll be right there."

When she turned her own smile on Bruno, it quavered before it held. *I love you too.* Then she grinned. *Don't worry so much. I'll give you the chance to show me just how happy you are to have me back in your arms.* She winked. *And in your bed.* She chuckled. *My bed, whatever. You'll have the opportu-*

nity to prove just how much you want me. And it'd better be a whole fuck-ton.

He growled and felt his nostrils flare. *More than that. Let me show you how much right now.*

She laughed like a melody, a balm to his heart. Then she kissed him again, and before he processed that she was finished with her goodbye, she turned and walked back toward Meiling and the wizards.

The short distance between them felt like a chasm.

But now that he was certain he couldn't stop what was about to happen, he pulled himself together and focused on doing whatever he could do to help her.

He was a beta, with a wolf as strong as any alpha's. He'd tear through anyone and anything to protect his mate. He only hoped Cassia came near him so he could show her what he thought of her snatching Naya and nearly killing her, of the lies the immortal told that kept his mate from living the kind of life she deserved.

Clove appeared at his side, accompanied by a man and woman who looked enough like her to suggest they were her parents. She elbowed him, one of her typical greetings. "Drop the worry-wart face, dude. It's unbecoming. Makes you look constipated."

He scowled at her.

"Though don't get me wrong, I'm pretty sure Naya would still want to jump you even if you wore a brown paper bag over your head."

"Clove," the woman beside her admonished.

Clove waved her away. "You keep forgetting I'm an adult now, Ma. I can talk however I want."

"Then you'd think you'd have motivation to sound intelligent and refined."

Clove rolled her eyes so exaggeratedly that Bruno was shocked her mother didn't notice. Perhaps the woman didn't want to. Having Clove as a daughter had probably frayed her patience over the years.

Clove's eyes fixed on Naya up ahead, she said, "Our girl's gonna be fine. Not even a crazy spell by two weird-ass mages or an even crazier immortal will be able to get to her. She'll kick their asses from here to next week."

Bruno raised a single eyebrow. "She'll kick the asses of a spell, two see-through wizards, and a woman who can't die? Is that what you're saying?"

"Yep. No doubt. Girl's got moves you never even heard of. Or imagined." She glanced at him. "Or wait, guess you've probably seen sides of her that no one else has. Speaking of, what's my girl like?"

"What do you mean, what's she like?"

She rolled her eyes again. "Are you really this

dense or are you just pretending? *In bed*, bro. Does my girl rock it in bed? I got a feeling she does. You know, she—"

"*Clove!*"

This time, it was Maverick.

"Don't you have something better to do than run your mouth off about things that don't concern you?"

As if Maverick weren't her alpha, and as if he didn't have a very fine point that Bruno himself was preparing to make, she said, "Of course it concerns me. Everything about Naya is my biz. She's my buff."

"What the fuck's a buff?" Mav asked, irritation morphing his question into an accusation.

"You know, a buffffff." When Mav and Bruno simply stared at her, she added, "B-F-F. Buff. Do I gotta spell it out for you, boys?"

"*Clove!*" her mom reprimanded in a sharp verbal smack. "That is your alpha you're addressing."

For the first time since Bruno had known her, the young woman blushed and tilted her head down. "Sorry, Mav. I get carried away sometimes."

He snorted, but sounded much less annoyed. "Just sometimes?"

Clove's parents stepped toward them, blocking Bruno's view of Naya. Her dad said, "Sorry, Alpha. Clove doesn't think before she speaks."

Whatever self-awareness had been affecting

Clove disappeared in a flash. Eyes narrowed, she opened her mouth to speak—

And a flash of gold-and-blue light pulsed out into the clearing, momentarily blinding them.

Bruno didn't stop to think, he ran toward Naya—and slammed into a wall of light that was as solid as if it were built from bricks.

"*Puta mierda,*" he grunted as he rubbed at the shoulder that had taken the brunt of the impact. How had he not realized the wizards had already begun? He should have never allowed himself to become distracted! He knew better than to give in to his emotions, no matter how intense or potentially justified they were.

He wasn't the only one to run headlong into the light. Shifter after shifter attempted to get to Naya, with the same result.

"Halt," Maverick commanded, and everyone stopped.

Naya and Meiling, along with Albacus and Mordecai, stood in the middle of a circle of light that stretched as high as the trees. A rush of air whipped their long hair around their heads; the beads of the brothers' braids clinked together jarringly.

Facing each other, the sisters held hands, their eyes clamped shut as their hair lashed against their faces with enough force to sting.

The mages' mouths were moving, but the wind whistled and howled, swallowing up their words. Their lips formed the same shapes, telling Bruno that, whatever spell they were chanting, they were doing it as one.

The wall of blue and gold crackled as if it were made of flame, before it shrank and concentrated into flicking tongues of golden-blue fire.

Just as Bruno was readying to jump over them, the tendrils of magic licked across the ground to race up Naya's and Meiling's bodies, electrifying them, propelling their hair to stand on end.

Bruno leapt just as the remaining flames of magic roared and surged upward, closing up the wall that kept him from his mate.

Brother Wolf yipped and Bruno growled as the barrier smacked him back, landing him on his ass.

Jumping back up, he snarled, deep and viciously, at the cage of light that kept him out. On a rational level, he understood he shouldn't interfere during the spell, but his wolf vibrated with frantic energy, pushing Bruno to protect Naya from the intangible forces that held her in their thrall.

The golden-hued blue glowed around Naya and her sister, expanding outward with a flare of light that caused them to throw their heads back with a strangled cry.

Brother Wolf howled, and this time it was a battle cry. Bruno studied the translucent wall separating him from Naya, waiting for his chance, any opportunity, to spare her from pain.

"Bruno," someone said from behind him, latching their hands on his arms and attempting to hold him back.

He whipped his arms out of the person's grip and turned to gnarl at them.

Clove held up her hands. "Whoa, asshole. Calm the fuck down. You're not yourself right now."

Brother Wolf was seconds from pushing his way out through his flesh. If the man wouldn't protect his mate, then the wolf would.

"Look at me," Clove said.

Bruno snarled.

"Naya's okay."

"Like hell she is. She's hurting."

"No." She turned him, and he felt how unwieldy his body was. The rational side of his mind could tell that he was overreacting, but the wolf in him refused to calm.

Bruno was a beta; he knew better than this.

But even as he thought it, his every muscle fought to intervene, to step between Naya and whatever the mages were doing to her.

"Check it out. She's fine," Clove said. "Breathe. Down, boy."

Naya's face was scrunched in discomfort, but not pain, he decided. Brother Wolf stopped howling, pacing the walls of Bruno's body instead.

The glow of the brothers' magic was looping between Naya and Meiling, cycling across their linked arms over and again, their long hair haloed a couple of feet around their heads.

Bruno forced himself to breathe, focused on accessing more of the man than the wolf, seeking that control that named him beta of the Andes Mountain Pack. He made himself notice how strong Naya was. How determined even amid uncertainty. How fierce. She was incredible. A warrior.

Get your shit together, Bruno. This won't do, he told himself, and the words finally began to sink in. He'd never reacted like this before, not without an immediate physical threat.

Then again, he'd never had a mate before.

"That's it," Clove said, and he grunted at her, not appreciating the fact that wild, over-the-top Clove was the one keeping her cool right now instead of him.

Naya's head tilted back up so it sat straight atop her neck, and she opened her eyes, singling him out amid the bevy of shifters.

Her eyes glowed violet—the same hue as Meiling's now that she wore the immortal's likeness.

I'm all right, Naya told Bruno. *I feel fine.*

Bruno's wolf perked his ears toward the internal voice of his beloved. Bruno felt like he could finally pull in a full breath again.

Clove whistled softly beside him. "Damn. Her eyes."

But Bruno didn't much care about her eyes right then. Yes, they were the wrong shade, but he could still make out the mate bond through them. He could feel the link that connected her to him, intact.

His shoulders and spine relaxed. His thighs unclenched.

The flames of the spell began to dissolve.

The brightness of the wall dimmed, the glow softened, until finally the magic disappeared entirely.

As a whole, the spectators sucked in relief.

Bruno ran toward Naya.

"Stop!" Mordecai barked. "Don't touch her yet."

Though Bruno the man was once more in control, he snarled at the mage's order that kept him from touching her, from reassuring himself with all his senses that she was unharmed.

"Wait a moment," Albacus said, more gently now that Bruno had stopped running.

"We must verify that the exchange between

Naya and Meiling is sealed and unable to jump to anyone else."

Meiling faced them. "It's done. I can feel it and I'm sure. And..." She waggled her brows. "It worked."

Naya smiled, and never had Bruno witnessed a more determined, ferocious expression. It was the look of a man-eater focusing in on its prey. "Oh yeah it worked," she said, loudly enough that everyone there could hear. "I can feel the immortality magic inside me. And..." Her grin grew until her teeth showed. "I can feel Cassia too."

"Oh?" Albacus said. "That's unexpected."

"I have her magic now. I can sense the other parts of it, just like Mei can."

"She's close," Meiling said.

"Very close." Naya cracked her neck, her back, and her knuckles, swinging her arms at her sides, warming up. "Time to kill a bitch."

"That's right," Meiling said in a voice as cold as steel on a winter night. "With the two of us joined like this, she won't see it coming."

"We'll take her down before she figures out what's going on," Naya said, face stoic. Resolved.

Murderous.

After a rallying cry of support from the crowd, Bruno asked the wizards, "Will the immortality magic they possess protect them from ... an ordinary shifter death?"

The mages exchanged a look, then Mordecai answered, "The immortal only shared a small portion of her power with Meiling, and we redistributed it across the two of them. But—"

"But," Albacus picked up, "even a trace amount of the immortal's magic—"

"And the sisters have more than that."

"They do. Even a small bit should be enough to allow them to extract the other woman's power."

"To pull her magic to join theirs."

"You see," Albacus said, "magic of a certain type wants to form into one whole. It's the way of all magic. It seeks to unify when it has originated from one source."

"And in this case, it must have. Whenever Cassia was made immortal, it was one spell or one event that must have caused her change."

"So once Naya and Meiling are in position to draw the immortal's magic to them," Albacus said, "it should willingly and easily come to them."

"And hopefully by the time the immortal realizes what's happening—"

"It will be too late for her to reverse the flow of the magic. Once it picks up momentum, it will continue in that direction unless a much stronger opposing force pulls it the other way."

With both gnarled hands, Mordecai pointed to Naya and Meiling. "This means that you have to hit her hard and fast, and pull that magic out of her without delay."

"The slightest hesitation or pause could be the determining factor of this battle. You must strike hard, fast, and without mercy," Albacus said.

"Oh, don't worry about that." Naya's voice was like a blade sharpening against stone. "She hasn't earned mercy. She hasn't shown it to anyone else. I'll show her none."

"Not even a little," Meiling said to a chorus of encouraging cries.

"Get her," they said. "Kill the bitch." And, "Wipe her out before she hurts anyone else. She's a murderer."

Naya and Meiling lined up side by side, shoulder to shoulder, and though they were weaponless, the determined slant of their eyes and mouths spoke volumes.

With any luck, Cassia wouldn't anticipate what they were up to.

The women had trained all their lives for a challenge such as this one.

The time for fear, doubt, and hesitation was over.

Bruno was the first to step in line behind Naya and Meiling. Their roles as saviors had changed, but their mission was still to save them all.

He'd fight to protect both of them until the end.

Whatever that looked like.

He, too, had trained all his life to defend those he'd sworn to protect.

Like them, he was all in. They were heading to war...

CHAPTER THIRTEEN

CASSIA

SINCE SHE'D DISEMBARKED from the private jet that delivered her from France to the United States, she'd hardly stopped traveling, fervent in her drive to find Meiling. Even after Cassia realized Meiling was making her way to Naya, it had taken several days to hone in on the girl's trail. But once Cassia had, tracking her became simple. Too easy, really. Grand Master Ji-Hun was deluded in thinking he taught his pupils the art of defense. Or offense. The vampire masters had deceived her into thinking they ran a secure operation. Their monastery was a joke. Superstitious interpretations of mysticism and unrelenting discipline were not a martial art, no matter what they called it.

Cassia craved a challenge, a worthy adversary. Meiling was none of those things. She forged a path as evident as breadcrumbs, outlining her journey across forests. With the enhanced senses of her wolf, Cassia followed the scent of her prey with the kind of focus and efficiency that would have normally delighted her.

But whenever she thought of Meiling, she landed on images of Édouard soon after, and the needless death of her favorite servant was like an anvil she carried on her back, diluting the enjoyment of the hunt. All Cassia had dreamt of for decades was the feel of tracking, hunting, killing, *feasting*, of being fully in tune with a new, previously untapped kind of power. Now that she was doing all these things, their taste was bland, never fully satisfying.

Another reason to make Meiling pay. And soon.

The girl was only a day away by foot, less than an hour by air. What was better, she was with Naya. Now that Cassia was close, she could tell both girls were heading away from pack territory. Out into the open. Insects flying straight in the direction of Cassia's sticky web.

Several times, Cassia had attempted to tap into her longstanding connection to the alpha. She'd knocked on the door to his mind, the one that had never been closed to her before, not since she first set it up so long ago, but it didn't budge. After all this time, had Maverick finally realized he was a spy of his own precious pack? That he was the greatest traitor to them all? If he had, the brute of a wolf shifter didn't possess the skills to lock her out. But those oddly powerful wizards she'd faced down in China likely did...

Regardless, Cassia hadn't survived this long without being resourceful. Her wolf was new to her, *sì*, but her connection to the air element was centuries old. No matter what form Cassia took, she could still read the air around her. The information it provided extended far beyond even her wolf's enhanced sense of smell. The data was vague, undefined. It couldn't tell her what Maverick would have so plainly stated. It didn't *think* how people did. However, what it provided was sufficient.

Meiling and Naya were traveling toward Cassia, accompanied by other creatures, possibly even the two translucent mages. Headed directly to her.

Once they reached her, they wouldn't be walking away from the fight she'd bring them. She had an advantage none of them had, not even those annoying wizards, whose attacks had incapacitated her in a way no others ever had. No matter what they did to her, what spells they used, or what artillery they pointed her way, she alone would get up, over and over again. There was no way they could end her, and near infinite manners in which she could kill them all. She hoped Meiling and Naya were traveling toward her with a whole fucking army. She was ready for them.

Cassia threw her head back and howled into the dusk of descending night. Again, she drew breath and let the anguished cry of her soul ring free. The girls had taken something precious from her. Édouard had been a balm to her heavy heart over the last several centuries.

Her beast picked up on a nearby pack of wolves —the non-supernatural kind. Their scents and yips were agitated before they ran in the opposite direction—smarter than the shifters, who drew closer to their deaths with every step.

Cassia howled again, scented a deer, and tore after it.

The need to kill was already pumping through her veins. No ordinary prey would satiate it. But as she dug her claws into the fleeing deer, raking the flesh around the fluffy white underside of its erect tail, and sank her maw into the hot meat, she thought, *A perfect appetizer*.

Next up, the main meal—many, many courses— then dessert.

Cassia would have her revenge before the night was over. No taste was ever sweeter.

CHAPTER FOURTEEN

NAYA

THEIR PARTY WAS SO large that they sat in double rows around a single campfire. After confirming both with Naya and Meiling that Cassia was far enough away that she wouldn't spot it, Maverick had given the order. "It'll boost morale," he'd said, though it wasn't as if they'd be roasting marshmallows and singing *Kumbaya*.

The night air was thick with anticipation. Shifters sharpened their blades and cleaned their guns, making sure the magazines were loaded with the same silver bullets as the last time they'd checked. Conversations were either tense and abrupt, or raucous and concerning anything but the looming threat they drew nearer to with each day of travel.

It was their second night out searching for

Cassia. Naya and Meiling didn't sense the immortal with the precision of a tracking device. Rather, it was a general sense of direction and proximity.

Based on the progress the woman was making, and the fact that her path was more or less a straight line that avoided roads, she was traveling as a wolf.

In a stolen skin.

They still had no idea what kind of reinforcements she might be traveling with. To find out, Maverick had sent their scouts out in all directions; that was why he and his beta kept glancing at their cell phones. They'd put out the word with all the packs in the Americas to notify them of news of the woman or any of the other immortals in the Five. All the packs together formed a network of information. If anything suspicious was happening, they'd know of it. If hunters were on the move, they'd be informed of that too.

Naya and Meiling compared observations and concluded they were within fifty miles of the woman. They'd marked a fat red circle on a map for Maverick to see, and he'd sent more scouts out to close in on the area.

But no one was to approach her. No one was allowed to betray their presence. Mav's orders were to observe and report only. They had only one chance to kill Cassia—and it was possible they didn't even have that. They had to lean into every advantage.

That meant relying on the element of surprise.

If they were lucky, Cassia wouldn't see them coming. She wouldn't scent them or hear them.

Now that they were close, Maverick would take precautions, leaving a certain percentage of their company back at intervals. They'd be nearby if they were needed, but not close enough to tip their hand.

They hoped.

Naya sat on a felled tree, Bruno on one side of her, Meiling on the other. Clove was somewhere up in the trees, surveilling the makeshift campsite. Naya hadn't seen her in a couple of hours.

Bruno's thigh was pressed against Naya's. He squeezed her leg. "Ready to turn in? I'll keep watch."

Of course he'd keep watch. The man had barely closed his eyes over the past week.

She cast a longing glance at the row of tents behind them. There were fewer assembled today than there'd been the night before. No one was doing much sleeping, and if they did, it wasn't for long. Two-thirds of their group was traveling in their wolf forms. The remaining third traveled in a car-filled caravan, a concession to the few werewolves among them, along with a need for ready supplies.

The full moon was still a few days off, but Naya

already felt its weight as it loomed against her consciousness. Before long, the pain would seize her once more and her wolf would emerge. For three whole days she'd be useless in a fight against the immortal.

They had to find her. Tomorrow. No later.

Naya pointed her gaze up at the moon overhead. Bright and pregnant.

"I'll go sleep soon," she finally told Bruno. "But not yet. My mind's still spinning. I don't think I could get it to shut off yet."

Unlike him, however, Naya was forcing herself to rest. Their company might be filled with soldiers who'd fought hunters all their lives, but none of them could neutralize the threat Cassia posed.

That was all on the two sisters.

The wizard brothers traveled with them, often deep in conversation with each other, considering, and later discarding, a host of ideas.

In the end, the plan remained the same. Everyone but Naya, Meiling, and the mages would fall back when they came upon Cassia. The sisters would get the jump on her and pin her down long enough to perform their own version of the Kiss of Death—only they'd be drawing her immortality magic out through her breath, just as Cassia had attempted and failed to do with Meiling.

Relieved of her immortality, any one of them could end her. There was a line of shifters jockeying for the chance to be first.

Naya and Meiling didn't plan on allowing anyone else to have that particular honor.

The hundred or so wolves that traveled with them, along with Zasha, Quannah, and Boone, were there to support in whatever way they could, and to attack whatever army Cassia might be mobilizing.

The immortal was headed straight for the heart of Rocky Mountain Pack territory. There was no way she was coming alone. Not when she had to know there were several hundred fierce wolf shifters anticipating her arrival.

If all that should fail, Albacus and Mordecai had some backup plans involving ancient spells. They said they "might" work, but neither sounded too confident about their chances.

The ultimate safety of the entire supernatural community for many generations to come sat squarely on Naya's and Meiling's shoulders.

Bruno draped an arm around her and pulled her close in the cool night. "How are you feeling, *peligrosa?*" he asked. Even over the crackling fire, the scraping of metal, and constant conversation, every word they shared could be heard.

"I'm fine," Naya said. "Feeling great, actually. Glad this'll be over soon."

You look tense, he continued through their private connection. *Why don't we slip into the farthest tent, and I'll ... relax you.*

She looked over at him, arching an eyebrow. *Oh? That's a tempting suggestion...*

I aim to please.

Boy, did the man ever succeed.

As optimistic as Naya was, there was a substantial chance that nothing would ever be the same again after they encountered Cassia.

She grabbed Bruno's hand and was half out of her seat when Meiling tugged on her sweater.

When Naya looked over her shoulder at her, at first all she noticed was the strand of light, the color of the moon, that connected the two of them. Whatever spell the mages had performed to join their energy bodies, it had certainly worked. Naya, who only saw energy as a visible force on rare occasions, hadn't been able to stop seeing the bonds that linked her and her sister.

"Naya," Meiling whispered, "do you feel that?" Orange flames reflected in her odd violet eyes, heightening the warning of danger. "Feel what?" Naya asked.

"Cassia," Meiling breathed, so that it was barely

a rush of air.

A dozen shifters glanced in their direction, no doubt perking their ears. Renewed tension swept in a circle around them. Bruno stepped beside her, waiting, alertness wafting off him.

Naya felt all of that. But she didn't feel what Meiling was talking about.

She sat back down and closed her eyes, searching within herself for the immortality.

Unlike the magic of her werewolf, the immortality wasn't feral or passionate; it didn't have a will of its own, wanting to break free of its cage to run wild and free. It simply ... was, as if it were nothing more than a fact of life.

Once Naya connected to the steady hum, like that of a purring engine, within her that was the immortality magic, she pushed it outside of her, intending for it to link to its match.

It did. Within seconds, Naya's chest tightened as she felt the woman who housed the corresponding magic.

"Oh *fuck*," Naya muttered, and only after a series of exclamations from the others did she realize she'd spoken too loudly.

It didn't matter. They'd all know within minutes anyway.

She opened her eyes and stared at Meiling.

"She's moving again. And way too fast."

Meiling nodded, a beanie holding her dark hair in a tight sheet around her face. "That's what I feel too."

Naya faced the fire, blinking, thinking. "Oh my God." She whirled back around to face Meiling. "She must be fucking flying."

Mei's mouth was pressed into a grim line. "I think so."

Bruno was already stepping away, seeking her alpha.

"That must mean..." Naya shook her head to clear the path for the correct conclusions. They still knew too little about their enemy, dammit! "If she's flying, then she can't have anyone with her. Or at least, she's leaving them behind."

"Yes. But vampires are fast. They could cover ground quickly and catch up to her soon."

"That's true." Naya absently rubbed at her cheeks while she considered. "And she seems to always have a posse of vamps nearby."

Bruno's hand rested on her lower back as he returned with Maverick and River in tow.

"What's going on?" Maverick asked right away.

Naya glanced at Meiling. "Cassia's on the move. She's heading straight toward us, and she's getting closer so fast that it can only mean—"

"That she's motherfucking flying," Mav said in a grumble that expressed exactly how unfair it was that their adversary had this skill and they didn't.

"It's the only thing that makes sense," Meiling said.

"On the plus side," Naya added, "if she has her crew of obedient vampires with her, then she's leaving them in the dust."

"Or she might've ordered them to run as fast as they can to keep up," Mav said. "They'd probably still fall behind, but not by much."

Depending on their age and stamina, vampires could sustain blurring speeds for long enough periods to be a concern.

Maverick brought his hands to his hips and stared at the ground for a few moments before broadcasting to the entire Rocky Mountain Pack via the telepathic link:

Listen up, everyone. The immortal's on her way to us now.

Only the fire crackled in the sudden silence that descended over the night. Not even the crickets dared disrupt the tension that fell across their gathering like a smothering blanket.

If you're back on home land, Blake will tell you what to do. Stay sharp and alert. We can't be sure the immortal is acting alone. All of those unable to defend our home should head to the bunker now. Listen to your wolves if they warn you of danger. No matter what, stay safe and watch each others' backs.

Maverick studied the many wolves sitting around the fire, along with those emerging from tents and the surrounding forest.

The rest of this is only for those of you here. The immortal was fifty miles away. She's heading in our direction again now, but fast. She's flying.

A wolf in the circle stood from his seat to say, "Fuck her."

Yeah, that about sums it up. Unless something changes, we're going to war. Tonight. Right now. You all already know what to do. Weapon up. Hold your positions. Carry out your part in the plan. There'll be no sleep for any of us tonight.

He paused. *Watch your six, wolves. We're family. Let's all make it out of this one alive. Give it all you've got. Let's color the sunrise with the blood of a nasty immortal.*

Quiet cheers of agreement went up, no less rallying for their controlled volume.

Mav looked at River. "Update Zasha, Quannah, Boone, and the mages."

Then Mav turned to Bruno with an eyebrow raised in question as River darted off.

"No need," Bruno said. "I can guess at what you said. It's time to fight."

Maverick palmed him on the back. "That's right, man."

The alpha and Bruno exchanged a heated look, before Mav nodded at whatever silent understanding passed between them. Then he clapped Bruno again on the back and faced Naya and Meiling, who both now stood.

"How much time would you guess we have?" Maverick asked.

Mei closed her eyes to better feel the connection to the immortal, but Naya didn't have to this time.

Her breath caught as the invisible string that linked the sisters to Cassia vibrated, like the immortality magic could actually be excited about coalescing back into one whole.

Cassia was closing the distance between them quickly. She was already too close.

The tie between them was strong and growing more potent as the seconds passed.

"We have twenty minutes, tops," Naya said. When she heard the words, her intuition confirmed their veracity.

The immortality magic inside her wasn't talking to her in ways she recognized, but the surety was there nonetheless.

Maverick pinched his bottom lip between two fingers while he began circling the fire. The many shifters near them jumped up from their seats on tree stumps and ran off into the trees. Others disassembled tents and packed up the limited camping gear they'd laid out with the efficiency of soldiers used to being called into battle with seconds' notice. Cars started up in the distance, then peeled away.

Mav was ordering them all to fall back.

But did they still have the element of surprise if Cassia was headed straight toward them? Had she somehow received news of their positioning? Of their plan, flimsy as it was?

"This is also the route she'd take if she were heading to your pack's territory," Bruno said, as if reading her mind. "It doesn't mean she knows we're here."

"But it also doesn't mean she *doesn't* know."

He frowned. "No, no it doesn't."

Scowling while her mind wandered, Naya began warming up, stretching her arms and legs before stepping away from the others to do lunges and squats and throw punches into the air.

She could only hope that Cassia would give her a chance at a fair fight. Without the immortal's ability to control the air, Naya would bet she could take her. Naya would bet on Meiling too.

But the upcoming confrontation wouldn't be fair, and she and Meiling were as outmatched as the legendary David to Goliath.

"Here," Meiling said, drawing Naya's attention. Her sister with the dark hair and almost impossibly beautiful face held a sword in its scabbard out to her, hilt first.

"It's one of my favorites, a *dao*," Meiling told her as Naya accepted the offering. The weapon was a Chinese saber, curved, comparatively short, with a one-hundred-percent lethal single-sided blade.

"What about you?" Naya asked, sweeping her gaze up and down her sister.

As usual, Meiling's body was covered in an assortment of blades. They were strapped to her arms, thighs, and back.

But she had no sword.

"Don't worry about me. I'd rather make the kill up close and personal." Meiling smiled viciously, those cherry-colored lips parting to reveal teeth.

"Okay, thanks," Naya said. "It's a beautiful sword." A long line of symbols were etched into the blade in an elegant filigree.

Though Naya had a sidearm strapped to both thighs, loaded with silver bullets, she doubted she'd be using either. And the hunting knife attached to her arm was intended for close combat.

Naya laid the scabbard aside and moved through a few practice attacks, familiarizing herself with the shape and weight of the *dao*, and by the time she looked out at their surroundings again, the fire was doused, the tents and other camping gear were gone, and only Bruno, Maverick, River, and the wizards stood around them.

"What about Zasha, Quannah, and Boone?" Naya asked.

"They're leading the reinforcements," Maverick said. "How much time do we have left?"

Naya connected through her mind's eye to the rope that bound her and Mei to Cassia. It was strung tight, bright and pulsing.

She swallowed, then looked at Meiling, who nodded.

Naya sheathed the sword and strapped it around her waist, patting it. "I hope I get to behead her with this baby." Then, "We have less than ten minutes. Just enough for a quick pee break."

Nothing could interrupt her concentration when it mattered most, and it might be her last chance to empty her bladder for a while.

When Naya stepped away, Meiling followed, and once they returned Bruno was waiting, staring at Naya as if memorizing every one of her movements.

I'm coming back to you, she said through their mate bond, praying she was telling the truth.

I know, he said, but his smile was forced, and he couldn't quite conceal the worry dampening his brilliant eyes, the color of the sea and forest all at once.

Naya walked over to him and kissed him without warning. His arms instantly wrapped around her, pulling her tightly against him, encasing her in his warmth, his scent, in all that was him. *Mate.*

He growled into their kiss. Possessively.

Going from zero to sixty in a split second, his mouth consumed hers as if it were the last time. Heat flared up and down her body despite the dangers threatening them. Desire raced through her in a feverish rush, momentarily leaving her lightheaded.

And before she'd had even close to enough, he softened the kiss, as gentle as if it were imagined, then ... stepped back.

Instantly, she longed to wrap herself around him. To touch him again. To feel him close.

His eyes blazed into hers. *Te amo, peligrosa. Come back to me in one piece. I need all of you.*

She aggressively blinked away a sudden surge of need, nodded, and mouthed, "I love you."

Then she met eyes with her alpha and her beta. They'd follow at a discreet distance so Cassia wouldn't see them. The rest of their backup would be close behind. Naya flicked a final glance at Bruno—the way his gaze seemed to devour her, his every instinct urging him to remain at her side. His fists were clenched at his sides, his neck corded, his thighs so tight the contours of muscle were visible through his jeans.

Ignoring every instinct that urged her to remain with her mate, Naya tightened the shoelaces on her running shoes and raced away, Meiling keeping pace with muted footfalls.

Albacus and Mordecai would follow, trailing through the thick trees to conceal themselves from sight. Once Naya and Meiling drew near enough to Cassia that she might spot them, they'd hide in the thick foliage and slopes around them.

Surprise was everything. They had to sneak up on Cassia before she could bend the air to her will and pin the sisters in place.

And the bitch was flying. As far out of their reach as she might get.

The challenge had gone from unreasonably difficult to near-on impossible.

But Naya had a lot to give to the fight. She was no longer the savior of future generations of werewolves, but she had the opportunity to secure the safety of all shifters. Tonight.

It was time for Cassia's reign of terror to end.

CHAPTER FIFTEEN

NAYA

DESPITE THE MOONLIGHT that attempted to filter through the trees, amid the long shadows where the sisters currently hid, the night was dark and heavy.

Albacus and Mordecai bobbed somewhere behind the young women, the same shadows swallowing their translucent forms, as if they were a part of the night itself.

"Do you see her?" Meiling whispered. Though Cassia was unlikely to be near enough to hear them, they weren't taking any chances on revealing their presence.

"I don't," Naya gritted out, tamping down frustration so intense she wanted to scream instead. "But she was just there." Naya pointed to an exposed ridge a hundred feet above them where the immortal had paused her flight to rest, her slim silhouette all but disappearing behind a handful of aspens. The woman again wore leggings and a tunic, and the billowing fabric of her shirt finally captured Naya's attention, signaling her location.

"I was looking straight at her." Naya spoke softly. "I don't get how I didn't see her fly away. I mean, she was *right* there one minute, gone the next. How's that even possible?" She squeezed the end of her braid before flinging her hair away. "*Fuck.* We're never gonna catch her at this rate."

"Don't say that," Meiling said right away, though her melancholy tone revealed she shared the same fears. "Surely we'll catch up to her soon."

Naya and Meiling had been running up and down the foothills of the Rockies, weaving through thick forests, and leaping across boulders and frigid streams for what felt like an eternity. In reality, it had only been an hour and a half, but that was plenty long enough to reveal the cockamamie nature of their plan, especially since Meiling was operating in a borrowed body. Cassia had been in good shape— lean, long muscles suggesting regular physical activity—but not in the incredible peak condition Meiling had. Though her sister wasn't complaining, she was having to push harder than Naya to maintain their speed.

Naya had been crouching, but now she allowed herself to sink heavily to the ground, sitting on her butt and hugging her knees. Her breath still came rapidly.

"We have to figure out something else," she said. "This plan's idiotic. We're just running all over the fucking place, hoping we manage to catch her. And oh, we've gotta do that without her noticing." She picked up a thin stick and tossed it heatedly into the brush. It made no more sound than if a mouse had skittered through, and the act did nothing to relieve Naya's mounting frustration. "There has to be another way to do this!"

"But there isn't," Meiling said, purposefully slowing down her breathing. "If she sees us coming, or senses us in any way before we can overtake her, we're finished."

"And how exactly are we supposed to get the drop on an immortal who can fucking fly?"

All the hope that had filled Naya when she and her sister had set off had dwindled until all that was left was a fierce and pugnacious determination. They had to put an end to Cassia. They simply had to— however they could, no matter how long it took them.

"She can fly, yes," Meiling said. "And that's certainly not easy on us. But if we track her long enough, surely at some point she'll stop to sleep. Or she'll need to eat or drink, something. That's when we'll pounce on her." She smiled darkly, baring her teeth, wolf-like. "Then we'll suck out her immortality magic and take turns ripping her to shreds. By the holy book, she'll pay for what she did to Li Kāng. To everybody. She'll pay and pay until she finally dies."

Naya stared at her sister. "Okay, then. But that part of the plan isn't the problem. Cassia deserves everything coming her way. If we have to chase her around until she wears out, who's to say we won't wear out first?"

"We're both fit and strong."

"Sure we are. But she's *flying*. We're running up and down mountains, half crouching as we go, trying to hide." Naya hesitated. "And you're not in your body. This you hasn't trained day in and day out for ages."

"That doesn't matter. Mind over matter. That's one thing the sacred book taught me the vampire masters couldn't ruin. Since I'm in this body, I'm aligning it with me, with the image I have of myself and how I can move. It's just how it's going to be. In this, I choose." Meiling sat next to her, fiddling with some pebbles, inhaling deeply. "So what are you saying? You want to give up? The immortal can fly, so that's it?"

Naya tsked and scowled. "Of course that's not

what I'm saying. I'd chase the fucking woman to the ends of the earth if I had to. I'm just pissed is all."

Meiling arched her brows. "You're just ... complaining? Is that what you're saying?"

Naya's scowl deepened. "Hell yes I'm bitching. The immortal is flying, and we're running around like we're little miniature toys she's messing with. It *enrages* me. Why does she get all the power when she's gonna do awful things with it? What about all the good supes in the world who actually might deserve it?"

Meiling tossed a stone, then another. They thumped softly among the foliage. "It's not our job to question how the universe works. It's only our job to follow our guidance to complete our role in this life as best as possible."

Naya blinked at her. "You really believe that?"

"I do." Her expression was serene. It was the first time Naya had ever seen that kind of peace on Cassia's face.

Naya stared at her some more, taking in the long dark hair all but disappearing in the darkness. But those violet eyes, they seemed to almost glow.

Finally, Naya shook her head, her breathing coming regularly now. "Well, good on you if you can Zen it out. I just want to rip Cassia's throat out. She killed one of our sisters. We didn't even get a chance to know her first. And why? Because for fuckwad Cassia it wasn't enough for her to be *immortal*. Immortal! No, she needed to also be a wolf shifter. I mean, come on. She deserves a death far worse than what we'll give her." Naya paused. "In our pack, we aren't about turning the other cheek. Maybe we aren't *an eye for an eye* either, but we believe in fairness, and not just karmic fairness either. Our pack isn't a bunch of monks like where you were raised."

Meiling stared off into the darkness, searching for any sign of movement. Cassia was nearby. They could both feel her proximity.

"The vampire masters teach inner peace. It's one of the fundamental lessons we are meant to master."

Naya smiled bitterly. "Good for you, then. I'm sure it's nicer to feel at peace with it all than what I feel. Cassia kept me from living a normal life. I've been her captive up until now, and what's worse, I didn't even know it. I thought I was some savior bullshit. Mei, she killed our parents."

"I know."

"Doesn't that get to you? We never even got to know them. You were raised with vampires, for fuck's sake. Surely that's not what our parents would've wanted. After what I saw at the monastery, it's a wonder you survived. Those vamps are almost as cruel as Cassia." Naya gave a bitter chuckle. "Almost. Cassia's so much

worse. She legit blew up Master Xiong. Exploded him."
Naya shook her head at the nightmarish memory. "Aw,
hell. You already know all this. Let's just ... Cassia'll pop
up again soon. She's got to be somewhere right around
us. We'll chase her until we manage to get the jump on
her. Then we'll kick her ass and all will be right in the
world. Rainbows and fucking butterflies."

Naya jabbed her running shoes into the rich
humus they sat on, and Meiling laughed.

Naya jerked around to look at her. "What's so
funny?"

"You. I can't wait to see you end Cassia. She
deserves everything that's coming her way. Trust me,
there's no amount of Zen or inner peace that's going
to keep me from doling out her sentence. Someone
like her doesn't deserve to live."

Naya hesitated, then asked, "Would you say the
same about the vampire masters of the Shèng Shān
Monastery?"

Meiling didn't have to think about her answer.
"I'll deal with them next."

Naya's brows arched. "Oh?"

"Yes. I've been thinking about it a lot since I left.
They claim to be stewards of the sacred book, of a
way of life. But they're charlatans, using all of us for
their selfish ends." She tossed another small rock that

wouldn't make much noise as it landed. "They aren't all that different from Cassia. And now that I'm free of their hold over me—"

"You can kick ass and take names. Or in this case, kill like the badass mofo you are."

Meiling chuckled. "Yes, something like that."

"First ... Cassia." Naya peered out into the expanse that opened up just past the cover of forest they were tucked into. "She has to be here. She feels so close."

"Too close."

"How could she've disappeared when I was staring right at her? Are we missing something? Maybe our tracking's not working..."

One of the wizards cleared his throat, the sound gritty like stones tumbling over a small waterfall. "I've been pondering this situation. Eh, she may be utilizing her control over the element of air to distort her image. I think that may be possible. Without understanding more about her powers, I can't be certain."

"Ohhhh, *oui*," the other mage said, sounding begrudgingly impressed. "What a good thought, brother."

Acid churned in Naya's stomach. She turned around, squinting to distinguish the mages from their dappled surroundings. "You're seriously telling us that she can make herself disappear?"

Mordecai jingled the runes he seemed to forever carry in the pockets of his robe. "Well, it's just a hypothesis, not a guarantee."

"No," I muttered. "We wouldn't want any guarantees on this forsaken mission, now would we?"

Of course, Naya full well understood it wasn't either of the wizards' faults that she and Meiling were running around like idiots all over the damn Rockies. It wasn't anyone's fault except Cassia's. They'd set out to do the impossible. What no one had been able to do in over a thousand years, though Naya had to imagine somewhere along the line, someone else had tried—and failed.

"I would cast my runes to be certain," Mordecai said

And Albacus interjected, "Nothing about the runes is certain, brother. How many times must I remind you of the fact?"

"Perhaps as many times as I must remind you that the runes, in expert hands"—Mordecai clinked them together in his pocket—"can suggest great secrets and understandings."

"*Can* being the operative word. They can also mislead."

Mordecai frowned and tugged on his long beard.

"I think we're past the point of taking risks, wouldn't you say, brother? But I won't throw the runes tonight. I'll need a light to see them, and any kind of illumination, no matter how slight, is a risk we cannot take."

So it was just a hypothetical suggestion, Naya thought, pursing her lips. *An idea we can't use to make our lives easier.*

Naya tuned out the brothers as they continued their animated discussion in hushed whispers. Meiling was constantly scanning their surroundings. Naya studied the shadows up on the ridge instead, certain Cassia had to be somewhere in plain sight. When she didn't find her there, she scanned the valley below them.

"All right," she whispered. "Let's do this." She turned, interrupting. "Guys, if Cassia is using her control over the air to make herself disappear, is there some magic you can do to counteract it?"

"Oh." Albacus chuckled. "Oh no."

"Definitely not," Mordecai added, in case I'd missed the uplifting nature of their answer.

"Great. Awesome," I said.

"We can perform spells that bend the air—" Albacus said.

"And even alter the refraction of light," Mordecai added.

Meiling spun. "Then why can't you do that now?

Couldn't you force the air to reveal where she's hiding?"

The wizards looked at each other, making *as if* faces.

Albacus explained. "We can't control any of the elements and give them the proper respect they deserve. Forcing them to do anything—"

"Is the essence of dark magic."

"Something we won't do."

"Well, not unless the end result is honorable and necessary," Mordecai said.

"And in that case," Albacus added, "the debate becomes nebulous."

"Something we don't have time for now."

Naya wasn't about to argue. The brothers did enough of it.

"If, however..." Albacus started back up.

"We knew what spell she's using," Mordecai said.

"Then that would be another story."

"Let me guess," Naya said. "You don't know what spell she's using."

"Not in this case, no," Albacus said. "Her immortality magic is muddling our readings."

"And we know too little about immortality magic to make safe assumptions," Mordecai finished.

Convinced the mages would be of no immediate use, Naya turned back around. After another scan of the forest, and the valley and mountains around them, she closed her eyes, tuning out the brothers' ongoing conversation and focusing instead on her breath—in and out, in and out—until she found a semblance of stillness.

Then she reached for the immortality magic within her and expanded her awareness to identify more of its kind. In seconds, Naya felt Cassia at the edge of her consciousness, a soft violet glow in the darkness behind her closed eyelids.

"She's still here," Naya whispered. "Somewhere up and off to the left."

If her mind's eye were a map, it would place Cassia up on that damn ridge.

Naya swept her gaze across the outcropping, once, twice, and then a third time—

"There!" She jumped to her feet while pointing into the distance, where what looked like a small twig from their vantage point was leaping off the edge of a ledge.

Where an ordinary human would plummet to the ground far below, Cassia crested and banked as if she were a bird riding the air currents.

When Naya sprinted off in that direction, whipping past tree after tree, Meiling was immediately behind her. Their plan might be ridiculous in that they'd have to get extremely lucky to catch the immortal this way, but it was the only working plan they had.

Cassia was too powerful. Too dangerous.

They had to play the long game and be there when the woman decided to come down to rest.

Adrenaline surged through Naya's veins. She could outlast Cassia. It would only take this once. A single slip-up and they'd nab her.

Naya would sacrifice everything she had to complete the mission. From the determined grimace on Meiling's face, she would too.

Their chances might not be high, but they were real.

It was a test of strength, endurance, and faith. Naya had trained all her life to ensure she had plenty of the former. And of the latter? Well, she had everything to live for now. She had two surviving sisters, a mate who rocked her world at every opportunity, and newfound freedom from the curse of her savior story.

That was worth believing in.

She pushed herself to run faster, harder. Cassia was heading in the direction of pack lands. If they didn't stop her first, she'd enter them soon.

CHAPTER SIXTEEN

NAYA

ANOTHER COUPLE OF HOURS PASSED, during which Naya and Meiling continued tracking Cassia, the mages floating effortlessly behind them. It was past midnight, probably around one in the morning. Over the past hour, Cassia had looped in smaller and smaller concentric circles, each time drawing nearer to the Rocky Mountain Pack's territory.

The immortal flew in the cloudless sky overhead, in sight unless Naya and Meiling were whipping beneath tree canopies or charging up hills to get her back in view.

As Naya ran, Bruno used their telepathic link to communicate with her, anxious for news of progress, which he relayed to Maverick. The closer to the pack's lands the immortal drew, the more frequent their requests for updates. So far, they'd all been the same: Cassia was still out of reach, there was no sign she'd come within range of attack anytime soon, and her vampire minions hadn't made an appearance—yet. This final fact was both reassuring and troubling at the same time. Why would Cassia be traveling without her vampires? Sure, Meiling had killed Édouard, but she still had plenty of other blood-hungry servant boys. Who would kiss her ass if they weren't around? When vampires could travel nearly as fast across land as she could through flight, there seemed no obvious reason for them not to be with her, not when she traveled with them everywhere else.

Their absence suggested that, either they weren't there, and in that case, fuck yeah, or they were there all right, just none of their crew of shifters had spotted them. Naya and Meiling could be running straight toward an ambush.

If Cassia could vanish in mid-blink, Naya wouldn't put anything past the immortal and her team of vamps. Naya wasn't inclined to trust that just because she couldn't see the vamps, they weren't there. Unease crawled along her skin like goosebumps.

Though Naya was burning energy as quickly as she could amass it, tension continued to ride her body. She was on edge. Something wasn't right. Her intuition niggled at her, but she couldn't decide if her guidance system was trying to tell her something specific or simply protesting this ridiculous chase that appeared to have no end. Either way, Naya couldn't stop running to discern the difference.

Meiling wasn't kidding when she said she trained hard. She and Naya had been running at top speed for most of three-and-a-half hours. She possessed the preternatural stamina of wolf shifters, but that wasn't simply a fix-all, not when she was in Cassia's body. Meiling hadn't been kidding with her whole *mind over matter* hogwash. Her breath came harder than Naya's, and her face was flushed a bright pink even beneath the moonlight, but Meiling was still fast enough to keep up with her.

Naya slid to a stop at the top of a squat mountain, hands at her waist, breathing heavily. Meiling jerked to a halt next to her.

"What is it?" she asked on an exhale. The closer Cassia flew to pack lands, the less distance they were willing to leave between her and them. "Is she finally taking a break?"

Meiling panted as Naya pointed and said, "Over there. You smell her? I think she's that dark smudge moving right now. By the really big tree."

"Oh." Meiling inhaled in obvious relief. "Thank the holy book."

"No doubt. I didn't think the woman would ever stop. I've had to pee for like an hour."

"Me too." She squirmed as if to prove her point. "Think you can watch her while I go?"

Naya nodded. There was no chance she'd lose sight of the immortal now. Not when she was in the valley directly beneath them, less than a mile away, walking toward a winding stream that sliced between slabs of rock.

This was what they'd been waiting for all night.

She finally stopped, Naya told Bruno. *She looks like she's gonna drink at a stream. We're moving in. Don't answer. I need to focus.*

Bruno didn't respond, but he'd received her message. Naya could feel the reception as easily as if it were traveling through a cell phone.

When Meiling returned, she kept watch while Naya relieved herself faster than she ever had in her life, and then took a moment to stretch out her hamstrings while they were stopped. Cassia might take off again, and they could be running for several more hours. It seemed the immortal was taking full advantage of the honed tool that was Meiling's body. They'd already run a marathon.

Cassia splashed water on her face ... then whipped her head around and up.

Naya and Meiling dropped to the ground.

Behind them, the wizards yelped softly and dove into a nearby tree.

Naya's heart beat impossibly loud as she pressed herself flat against the cold rock at the pinnacle of the mountaintop. "Did she see us?"

Meiling whispered, though Cassia was too far away to hear them. "I don't think so. But then why'd she look straight up at where we were?"

Naya closed her eyes for a moment. *Please don't let her have seen us. After all this, please.* She crawled on her belly until she could peek over the edge.

Her jaw tightened.

"What? What is it?" Meiling hissed from behind her.

Dammit!

"She's gone."

"She can't be. She was just right there. Maybe she's hiding."

"Either way, we're fucked. If she's hiding, then she saw us, and forget us being able to sneak up on her. If she's gone, then we have to start tracking her all over again. Though at least she won't have gotten far," Naya added miserably. Was she going to make them run all night long without water or rest?

"Connect to her again," Albacus said, his voice suddenly right behind them. Stones jangled softly in the night. Mordecai was nervous, playing with his runes.

Naya sighed. Of course it's what they had to do, but could they not get a break already? She closed her eyes, reached for the immortality magic inside her.

It popped up directly beside her ... moving rapidly in the direction of her home.

Naya shot to her feet. "She's heading right for the pack."

"Then let's go," Meiling said, moving already, but Naya held a hand out to stop her. Meiling arched her brows in question.

"I think it's time for a gamble," Naya said.

"No gambling. We're taking enough risks as it is. We have to get her tonight."

"Exactly. If she's this close to pack land and heading that way, it's extremely likely that's her destination."

"But why? If the bloodline story was just that, a story, why would she be hunting you down?"

"I have no idea. But you've been there with me too. Maybe she's hunting us both. She has before. She's literally the reason we exist."

Both sisters shuddered, then turned to look at the mages. Albacus shrugged. "Perhaps her story was a ruse for another interest of hers she hasn't disclosed.

Or maybe she was lying, and your blood is actually meant to save werewolves from extinction. I wouldn't count on her veracity. She might still have need of you."

Naya grimaced and looked back at her sister. "What a cheery thought. Anyway, I think it's time to stop following her around like her playthings and take the most direct route. This land has been my prison my entire life. I've roamed every nook and cranny of these mountains. She's taking the most direct route as the crow flies. If we follow her that way, we're gonna be going up and down a ton. Let's tear up the ravines instead. We'll make way better time and conserve energy."

"So we can kill her."

"Right. So we can kill the shit out of her."

"I think that's smart. Worst-case scenario, we lose her and have to start tracking her all over again. But she must be going to the pack complex."

"Where all the kids and elders are," Naya said, feeling her brow bunch with concern.

"Right. So we hurry."

All they'd been doing all night was hurrying, but Naya nodded anyway. They'd have to run faster than before, on tanks that were at least half empty.

"Watch for loose rocks. We'll be going through an old dry riverbed at one point."

"Anything else I should know?" Meiling asked while Naya tightened her shoelaces.

"Yeah, run like the wind."

Then Naya set off to do exactly that.

———

ANOTHER HOUR PASSED, during which Naya and Meiling ran full out, leaping over fallen logs, stones, and tree roots without slowing. They couldn't have traveled any faster.

Even so, Naya wasn't sure they were moving quickly enough. Once more, her intuition pricked at her senses as insistently as the sweat that ran down her body in tickling rivulets.

She'd feel better if she knew what Cassia was up to—or maybe she wouldn't. It wasn't like the immortal was just stopping by the Rocky Mountain Pack complex for a spot of tea and a nice chat in the middle of the night.

Naya slowed, then stopped at the top of a butte that ended in a steep cliff, which Naya had climbed several times, always with a harness and rope.

Bust Your Ass.

The route was aptly named for a couple of gnarly holds halfway up the rock face—or halfway down, depending—that challenged even the most adept climbers.

Naya looked to Meiling, who stood at the edge, peering over the side. "Now what?" she asked.

Naya held up a finger, closing her eyes again. It took mere seconds to feel the immortality magic linking them to Cassia.

Her brow furrowed as she opened her eyes, staring at Meiling. "It doesn't make sense. You check to make sure."

Meiling tracked Cassia with a similar resulting surprise. "She's behind us."

"But heading this way."

"She must've taken a break."

"Finally, a break," Naya said. "We can come at her from both sides and catch her."

"How?"

"We split up. I climb down, you go around the long way."

Meiling shuffled to gaze over the side. "No way. You can't climb down that! That's death."

Naya frowned. "No, it's not. I've climbed it a couple dozen times. I know the route."

"That's insane, Naya! You'll fall."

"I won't. I climbed down the back of Shèng Shān Mountain, remember? That was an unfamiliar climb, and way, *way* higher up. Also, way steeper."

"Yeah, *remember*? You fell and *died*."

"I only fell when I was almost at the bottom, and that was only because my wolf came over me. If not, I would've made it."

"I can't believe that."

"Believe it, baby. If I could do that, I can do this. This is a walk in the park in comparison."

"But what's the point of us splitting up? Shouldn't we stick together?"

"Yes, but going around takes longer, and I'm not risking losing her."

"You'll have to wait for me either way. You can't take her on your own."

"No, but I can delay her while you catch up," Naya said.

"Delay her how? By letting her kill you?" Meiling snapped.

"That's not the plan, no."

"Then what is the plan? You climb down. I run around. We meet up, trapping her between us? Then she'll know we're there and we'll have lost the element of surprise. This whole chase will have been for nothing."

"Not if the wizard bros can do some magic."

Naya and Meiling turned as one to consider them.

Mordecai and Albacus smiled dreamily at them.

"Well?" Naya said. "Can you do some sort of distraction magic ... or concealing magic ... stuff, or not?"

Albacus and Mordecai were the first mages Naya had ever met, and that was on purpose. As a rule, wolf shifters didn't mingle with practitioners of the magical arts. Too many of them dabbled in dark magic. Too many of them were unscrupulous mercenaries.

After a shared look, Albacus and Mordecai grinned, bobbing their heads to a melody of porcelain beads tinkling together.

"If you split up," Mordecai said.

"We split up too," Albacus said.

"I know a spell that will make you fade into the mountain surrounding you," Mordecai said. "If Cassia were to look carefully, she'd notice. The spell isn't perfect. It blurs. But..."

"But if she isn't paying attention, it will work," Naya said. "And she should have no reason to look at the route." Naya's heart sank. "Unless she scents me. She's a wolf shifter now. She'll be able to smell me coming a mile away."

Mordecai tapped his long nose, making his whiskers tremble. "I have a spell for that too. And..." He waggled his eyebrows. "If you fall, I can catch you and hover you down to the ground."

"I won't fall."

"Well, if you were to..."

"I won't. Especially not this time. Any noise might alert her."

Mordecai scratched at his beard. "True. But, just in case. So you know, I'll be there."

Naya nodded sharply. She certainly wouldn't turn away a bearded, robed, magical version of a belay system. What she wouldn't have given to have had him with her when she was descending Shèng Shān Mountain. He would have saved her a whole lot of pain—oh, and death.

Albacus slid forward, his feet invisible beneath his draping robe, which hovered an inch off the ground. "And I will accompany Meiling. I too have a few tricks up my sleeves." He shook both out for good measure, revealing gangly, pale arms beneath gaping fabric. "The least of which is concealing her scent. I can mask sound as well. I just need a little lead time on the spell, but I'll be working on it while this young lady gets her exercise."

"Oh, I think we've gotten our exercise in for the next month or so," Naya muttered, but didn't mind when no one reacted. They had better things to focus on.

She squeezed Meiling's shoulder. Though she looked like the immortal now, she still felt like *sister*.

"Be careful. If for whatever reason you should arrive before me, which you shouldn't, keep yourself alive until I get there."

"Same goes for you," Meiling said. "Be safe, and then let's kill a bitch."

Naya couldn't help the grin that spread across her face. "Your English just keeps getting better and better."

Meiling winked. "I have an amazing teacher."

Mordecai cleared his throat. "At a more opportune time, I'd beg to differ. The way youths talk these days..." He shook his head: more beaded chiming. "Not quite the sophistication my brother and I are used to."

Albacus palmed his brother on the back. "Ach, brother, you sound like Sir Lancelot. People have cursed and perverted languages since time began. It's how languages evolve."

"Is it evolution, brother? Or devolution?"

Naya rolled her eyes then stared at Meiling, who nodded.

While the brothers debated the pros and cons of their latest argument, Naya told Meiling, "There's a hiking trail just around that bend, behind that tree." Meiling turned to see where Naya was pointing. "Follow it all the way until you see Cassia. It should pass right by the general area where we're sensing her."

If only that feeling pinpointed her location exactly. But this information would still get them close enough. Assuming Cassia didn't take off in flight, or begin traveling in the opposite direction—or that she wasn't stopping to meet up with her vampire posse.

There were far too many unknowns, and only one imperative: kill her before she could hurt anyone else.

The risks were calculated and worth taking.

"See you soon, sister," Meiling said.

"See *you* soon," Naya said, hoping their words would prove true.

It would take both of them to incapacitate Cassia. Plus a little luck, possibly a lot of it, depending on how accurate the quibbling wizards were in their deductions on how to siphon immortality magic.

Without waiting for the mages to get into position, Meiling ran off, and Naya unhooked the sword Mei had given her and draped it to rest against her back, where it wouldn't be in the way. After a quick thought, she removed her sneakers, stuffed her socks inside them, and tied them onto the sword's sheath.

Far more precise to climb barefoot than in clunky shoes.

She lowered herself to her stomach, feet dangling into empty air, drew in several deep breaths, then inched over the edge, searching for her first hold.

Her toes scraped along the rock face until she found the first depression in stone. Then she felt for the next, and the one after that, until her entire body weight hung from her fingers and toes.

Her muscles were exhausted, but they were surely warmed up. Naya could complete a climb like this easily. She just needed to keep her thoughts in check. No worrying about how foolish it was to climb after running for so long, when muscle spasms and cramps might occur.

Simply one hold after another. One grip after the next.

Her prize was waiting below, too close to all she held dear in the world.

CHAPTER SEVENTEEN

NAYA

NAYA CLIMBED down the rock face as quickly as she was able, well aware that the clock was ticking against how long her muscles would cooperate the way she needed them to. And though Mordecai floated along a dozen feet away from her, his translucent form all but disappearing into the dark rock behind him, Naya didn't trust that he'd catch her if she fell. Nothing about the wizard brothers suggested a speedy response time, and a fall could happen so quickly that, by the time the accident registered, the climber was on the ground in a heap and a splat.

Just like Liv, she thought with a painful pang, the face of her client and friend coalescing in her mind, a halo of bright blood pooling behind the woman's head, eyes blank and unseeing.

Before the imagery could take hold, Naya shook

it away. Now wasn't the time for that particular regret.

She made it halfway down the cliff face before her biceps and forearm muscles began trembling. She'd figured it'd be her legs that would give first, counting on this probability. Most of the strength for her climbs derived from her legs; it was the way with most female climbers. She could push into her legs even when they were exhausted. But her arms? She needed precision with each and every handhold, especially when some of the protrusions she held on to were barely nubs.

Halfway down, at the first hold that gave the route its Bust Your Ass moniker, the shaking in Naya's left arm extended to her hand, causing her fingers to slip at the most crucial juncture of her descent.

Her left arm flopped away from the rock, and that momentum made her lose her footing. She didn't so much as breathe while her entire body dangled from the mountain, hanging only from her right fingers.

It perhaps took her a whole five seconds to remedy her position, cramming a knee-bar against an indent and clinging to the rock face like a monkey who'd suddenly discovered her mortality. Her breathing came too harshly; her arm shook harder than before, and worse, she had to release one hand-hold and then the other to rub her sweaty palms against her thighs. She could have really used a chalk bag right around then. She would have also taken a harness and rope, and while she was at it, a world that already came pre-established without a creepy, cold-hearted immortal.

Naya clung to the mountain longer than she should have and she knew it. *Move, move, move! Fucking move.*

She whipped past the final Bust Your Ass hold at dizzying speeds, refusing to let herself think about what she was doing, leaning instead into the moves her body could perform as easily as running.

By the time she made it to the base of the climb, her heart was thumping, she was sweating an unrea-sonable amount, and her nerves were shot to hell and back. But as her bare feet settled onto solid ground, and her leg muscles wobbled alarmingly, she didn't even allow herself to stop to rest. She used up a moment to remind herself of what was at stake, then shook off the close calls of the descent and got her shit together.

Though she wanted to verify with Mordecai that he was still masking her approach, she didn't dare ask at this stage. If Cassia had remained where Naya hoped she would, she was right around the bend, within earshot for a shifter of any sort.

Here we go.

The arches of Naya's feet ached, and pointed rocks had dug into her flesh on the way down. Still, she didn't pause to put on her shoes. Even a rustle could be enough to give away her position, depending on how well Mordecai's spell worked. He'd been mumbling indiscernible chants all the way down, but Naya wasn't taking any unnecessary risks. Better to be doubly protected from discovery than to become cocky at the home stretch.

She hoped with all she had left in her that it was the end.

As she tiptoed across the ground, hard dirt mixed with rock, she visualized making the turn and finding Cassia there, completely unaware, her back to Naya.

Naya rounded the bend ... and there stood Cassia.

Her vampire minions weren't with her.

But she wasn't alone.

An entire army of Rocky Mountain Pack shifters faced her down.

Dammit!

So much for the element of surprise she and Meiling had worked so hard to maintain!

Her heart sank until it beat along with the pulsing in her sore feet.

But as Naya approached the scene, Cassia seemed to remain unaware of her. She didn't turn, and none of the pack wolves glanced at Naya, not even Bruno or Maverick, who were at the front of the line.

They were all protecting her position, Naya realized. They wouldn't give her away.

There was still a shot. Plus, they'd distract Cassia from Meiling's impending arrival.

Naya hoped, anyway.

When a few of the pack wolves gnarred at the immortal, Naya took the opportunity to draw Meiling's sword—gently, slowly, carefully, so that their snarls consumed the sound of metal on leather.

Without glancing at her directly, others in the pack noticed her intentions, joining the din by adding their own threats.

Naya padded on quiet footfalls while Cassia, though in human form, growled back at them.

By the time the immortal somehow became aware of Naya's approach despite Mordecai's assistance, Naya held the sword at an angle for attack.

As Cassia spun to face her, her lips pulled back

in a menacing snarl, all teeth, Naya swung the blade downward, slicing Cassia's head clean off.

Blond strands fluttered downward softly, like silent snowflakes. The head bounced once on the ground, then stilled, amid a spray of arterial blood from the remaining stump of a neck.

Naya swallowed down a surge of bile as she stared at Cassia's head—her very own fucking face! The dao cut cleanly, exposing a cross-section of bright bone, bloody meat, and thick veins.

Unblinking, her disembodied head stared back at her.

Vomit shoved into her throat; she swallowed down the acid.

How many people beheaded their own reflections?

Tearing her gaze away from the head, one of its cheeks partially pressed to the ground, Naya waited for Cassia's body to drop. Only it didn't.

The headless body stalked Naya. *Stalked her.* Without any visible loss of strength.

Now, Naya hadn't expected to kill Cassia, even though Meiling's silver blade would have ended any other shifter with a cut like that. But she sure as shit had expected a bloody beheading with a silver blade to at least slow her down and allow Meiling the time to arrive. Wolf shifters were renowned for their preternaturally rapid healing and for their ability to grow back limbs, even heads every once in a rare while—so long as the blade used wasn't silver. But nobody could bounce back from a beheading like this.

Dismayed cries rose from the pack wolves. Naya tuned them out. She wasn't the kind of woman who backed away from her problems. She prided herself on ramming them head-on.

But Naya had never been pursued by a headless naked woman who looked exactly like her.

She took several steps backward while absently registering Bruno's enraged howl and that he was charging toward them.

Since her throat was sliced apart, Cassia wasn't voicing any threats, but her body was crouched for attack, shoulders bunched low.

Naya had a straight-on view of Cassia's open neck—and the way the tissue was rapidly regenerating, pushing upward—growing like a fucking plant in one of those fast-forwarded videos that covered the progress of a few months in a single minute.

Cassia's neck was sprouting like a motherfucking shoot on steroids.

Panic threatened to seize Naya; she shoved it away with brutal determination.

Meiling wouldn't be long now.

Without tearing her gaze from the grisly scene in front of her, Naya squatted and gently tossed the sword to the ground, then drew both pistols from their thigh holsters and clicked off the safeties. She aimed both guns at the monster in front of her, sighted, and, double fisted, unloaded the entirety of both full magazines into Cassia's body. A total of twenty silver bullets sank into Cassia's regenerating head, heart, chest.

Cassia kept coming toward Naya like she just wouldn't stop, but then she staggered and fell to her side, chest heaving, breasts bobbing.

But her head kept growing.

The narrow shoot from before had enlarged until it was nearly the width of her neck. Raw red flesh pushed upward, and as Naya stared, equally trans-fixed as she was horrified, the repairing stump stretched and crunched, producing the beginnings of a mandible.

"Oh my fucking fuck," someone said, to several grunts of agreement, and it was only then that Naya realized Clove stood beside her in her human form. Bruno and Maverick stood on her other side. Bruno placed a hand on her back in silent support.

A commotion interrupted the heavy shock, and Meiling popped through the crowd of heavily armed shifters gathering around the impossible creature in their midst that was obviously immune to the silver poisoning that was lethal to the rest of them.

"I'm here, I'm here!" Meiling called, panting. She would have had to run the entire way to arrive this soon.

"Thank God," Naya said. "Her head's almost finished regrowing."

Meiling stuttered to a stop, Albacus floating through her before he could stop his forward momentum, a chagrined look coloring the patch of cheeks visible behind all that facial hair.

With eyes so wide Naya could make out the white all around her violet irises, Meiling gaped at Cassia.

"How...? What...?" Meiling shook her head. "Never mind. Just ... never mind."

"Shit, she's shifting," someone cursed, and Naya whipped her attention back to the immortal.

Bone, sinew, and flesh cracked. Cassia dropped to all fours, distorting, stretching, and shrinking in inhuman ways. Faster than should have been possible for someone so new to her second form, Cassia transformed into her animal, all without interrupting her regeneration. By the time her shift was complete, Naya was staring at a head that already resembled a wolf.

Naya faced Albacus and Mordecai. "Can we still do this with her as a wolf?"

The brothers tilted their heads this way and that in a caricature that spelled out *pensiveness*, then they nodded in unison.

"*Oui*," Albacus said. "It shouldn't change a thing. She'll still have the same energy signature, the same magical makeup. The wolf is coexisting with the woman."

"Precisely," Mordecai added. "Her immortality magic will remain the same. Nothing needs to change."

Except now either she or Meiling would have to press their mouths to jaws that could tear them apart.

Cassia's head was now a misshapen lump of pink flesh, like Silly Putty that was continually refining. Hair was growing, teeth stretching, eyeballs rounding in their sockets. Already several of the bullets lay on the ground around her body, and her torso was in the process of pushing out another couple. The flesh closed almost immediately after, the fur covering the tissue in an instant.

"We should just keep cutting her head off till it sticks," one of the shifters said. Another added, "I brought extra magazines. The silver'll get to her at some point." And yet another said, "After we whack off her head this time, we should set her on fire. That's bound to do something."

If only it were that simple...

The suggestions continued, equally useless in these special circumstances.

Naya turned to the mages. "How long will it take you to do your thing?"

They'd discussed it earlier and decided that the brothers would actively link the sisters together, so that while one performed the Kiss of Death, AKA Immortality Magic Removal, the energy of the one would be bolstered in every way possible by the magic and life force of the second. Naya was all about redundancy, given the impossibility of the task at hand.

"Merely moments," Mordecai said.

After a look at Meiling, who nodded her readiness at her, Naya said, "Then begin."

While the brothers linked hands and began chanting in Latin, Naya holstered her pistols and extended her own toward Meiling. When the sisters touched, Bruno and Maverick stepped back, and River yanked Clove away when she didn't move on her own.

Naya and Meiling lined up in front of Cassia's wolf, and as they did, Cassia staggered to her paws and stared back at them with eerie, glassy eyes that appeared flat and lifeless already in the deep of night. Dawn was still too far off to lighten the sky.

The chanting behind them grew louder ... and then the brothers stuttered.

A fierce wind erupted seemingly out of nowhere, tearing at their clothes, hair, and bodies so intently that Naya had to plant her tired legs and lean forward into the gust.

"*Merde*," Albacus cursed. "We must split forces, brother."

Mordecai didn't even respond, bearing down with a strength Naya hadn't realized he possessed, increasing the volume of his chanting as Albacus switched course mid-spell, and began working to counteract Cassia's control of the air.

"What do we do?" a shifter cried from behind them, but there was nothing any of them, not even their alpha, could do to take down Cassia and her magic.

Naya squeezed Meiling's hand. It was all on them. Together, the young women leaned into the lashing, punishing wind, and forced their way to Cassia.

Only then did Naya realize they'd need help keeping her jaws open while they sucked out her magic.

Unwilling to reveal their hand to Cassia, Naya

used the pack link, relaying her message through Bruno. There wasn't time.

We need someone to hold her in place and keep her jaws open so she can't hurt us.

Without delay, Mav's orders arrived. *River, Scooby, and Cleo, you hold her down. I'll hold open her jaws. If we need any help, rush in at will. All hands on deck.*

In a blur, River and Scooby pinned Cassia down, pressing all their weight onto her, their muscles bulging. Cleo pulled her hind legs out straight behind her, forcing the wolf off balance, down onto her stomach. The large wolf, the color of shadow, struggled, twisting her head to snap at the shifters behind her.

Maverick yanked her head around toward him, wrenching her jaws open with the strength of an alpha. Cassia tried to snap her jaws down, but Maverick had wedged his thick fingers in the back of her jaw, behind her teeth.

Cassia choked and snarled, but Naya refused to feel pity. It was a concept foreign to the immortal.

The chanting behind them grew louder, more fervent, more intense, and the wind diminished, only stinging Naya's skin instead of feeling like it was mere moments from peeling it off.

"Now!" Naya said, intending to be the one to

draw out Cassia's eternal life, but before she could get the word fully out, Meiling stepped forward, pulling Naya beside her, and lowered her face to the terrifying teeth, dripping rabid drool and foam.

Meiling didn't hesitate, and as she stretched her mouth wide and pressed her lips to Cassia's, attempting a seal, Naya saw the bonds of energy linking her to Meiling flare to life.

Whatever the brothers were doing was working.

Bright arcs of violet energy linked Naya to her twin and to the immortal. Like the electric power of a lightning flash, the light ran in a continual frenzy between all three of them.

At first, the immortality magic rushed in Cassia's direction, and Naya experienced her first real threads of fear.

But then Meiling doubled down, and Naya pulled her energy through her sister with all her might, and the flow of the power reversed.

Cassia's immortality magic was streaming into Meiling.

CHAPTER EIGHTEEN

CASSIA

FOR THE FIRST time since she killed her father nearly seven-hundred years before, Cassia experienced fear. Shock paralyzed her. Then when she renewed her efforts to stop Meiling and Naya, their combined strength was too much and she was already at a disadvantage.

No, no, no! The anguished cry echoed deep within her, though she didn't make a sound.

That brute of an alpha had her jaws stretched open so far she worried they might break apart, her wolf body clamped down so that she could scarcely move. Her joints hurt from the unnatural pressure, her muscles strained. The elegant, efficient beast that was her newly developed wolf felt wholly inadequate.

Tears pricked at her eyes, making even her

eyeballs sting—another first in longer than was worth recalling. It didn't much matter; her view of Meiling as the young woman pressed her mouth to hers was blurry, both due to the other woman's proximity and the rush of power leaving Cassia.

Leaving her for good, she feared.

Attempting to swallow and finding herself unable to, she screamed deep inside. Again, not a peep actually emerged from her being. Nothing was working as it should.

Cassia attempted to overlook the exasperating pain and discomfort to center herself enough to control the air element as she'd done thousands of times. But those *bastardi* of mages were chanting spells that were interfering with her ability to do what she'd done so easily before.

Either that, or it was her waning strength, a fact that was equally worrisome.

Suffocating, she could feel her immortality magic streaming out of her as if these bitch sisters were stealing her very breath. The ungrateful *puttane* wouldn't even exist if not for her! Their moronic parents would never have had them. They could barely figure out how to fit the pole in the hole without her help. Where was the fucking gratitude? She might as well be their bloody mother! More than two decades of life was better than never existing at all. How did they not see that?

How had things gone wrong so quickly?

She'd anticipated that the pack wolves would fight her as soon as she crossed their boundaries. She hadn't yet gotten to experience a true battle in her four-legged form, and she'd been looking forward to the battle. After all, if they hurt her, she'd simply regenerate, and in the meantime she'd get to deliver punishing blows.

But the ungrateful sisters had taken her by surprise. It shouldn't have been possible. It definitely shouldn't have been possible for the twins to figure out how to remove her immortality magic. That was Cassia's one invulnerable secret. Never, in her long life, had she whispered it to a single soul.

And yet ... here they were. It had to be the mages. The sisters were too stupid and naïve.

A strangled cry erupted from her throat, but the alpha only pulled her jaws apart farther. The asshole. When she got out of this mess, she was going to make an example of him and kill him in front of his wolves.

And then she was finally going to murder the sisters.

She'd lay waste to the whole pack.

No one messed with her, the great immortal.

She was the Kiss of Death. *Osculum Mortis.* *Filema Thanatou.*

She was the seed of legends and nightmares, a secret concealed in the shadows of the supernatural community. She moved like a whisper, like a prayer, ever out of reach.

These *girls* would *not* be the end of the Kiss of Death. That would be absurd.

Meiling pressed her lips to Cassia's wolf mouth with crushing pressure and slurped up more of Cassia's immortality magic.

All at once, Cassia became lightheaded, and her vision swam. She couldn't breathe despite how hard she pulled through her nose. Her throat constricted.

Only ... then she noticed it wasn't breath she was lacking, but rather she was experiencing the final dregs of her magic drifting through her ... and into Meiling. Into Naya. United against her.

Non è possibile, she thought in a panic, reverting to the modern form of her native tongue. *It's not possible*.

Only, obviously it was.

Cassia's heart squeezed so painfully that stars burst across her bleary vision. Every cell in her burned like she was on fire, as if she were coming apart at the seams. Lucid thought suddenly moved beyond her grasp; she reached for it, but it disintegrated like the wisps of a cloud. She was no longer the intelligent woman who'd strategized across centuries, making every move with a precise end game in mind. She'd become a writhing mess of pain, despair, and fury. A bloody pulp, a mere remnant of the woman she used to be.

Control of the air was beyond her reach. She was vulnerable, weak, spent.

When Meiling withdrew her mouth from hers, and Naya stepped up in her place, Cassia collapsed into the hold the alpha and his shifters had on her body.

She closed her eyes, unsure whether she'd ever open them again.

———

Naya

Cassia's large dark wolf hung limply in the hold of Maverick, Bruno, Scooby, and Cleo.

Naya took another step toward her. "Did she pass out?" She surely wasn't dead. Every silver bullet Naya had pumped into her body lay on the ground around them.

"Must be," Maverick said. "Did you two pull out all her immortality magic?"

Though Naya already knew the answer, she looked to Meiling.

Her sister wiped her mouth. "I think so." She paused. "Actually, I'm certain. We took it all."

Meiling squeezed Naya's hand, which she still held, seeming not to want to let go. Naya understood. That had been some dark shit.

Though Naya hadn't been the one sucking the magic directly out of Cassia like she was transferring an electric current through her, she experienced every bit of magic passing from Cassia to her sister just the same. Besides that, Naya could see violet energy flickering around inside Meiling. Some of it arced across Meiling's arm to Naya's.

But none of it circulated through Cassia. Not anymore.

The great immortal was in need of a change of title, stat.

Naya met Maverick's waiting stare. "She's fresh out. There isn't a speck left in her."

Naya met Bruno's eyes. They were luminous. Proud. Loving. She smiled at him. Now that Cassia was a mortal, she was no match for them.

In the background, Mordecai and Albacus' spells drew to an end, and a shocked silence swept across all of them gathered there.

Despite her determination, Naya hadn't been

certain she and Meiling would succeed. After all, Cassia had been *immortal*. Unkillable.

Now, she was just a beaten wolf.

Then Cassia's wolf form began to vibrate, then tremble. Her entire body shuddered violently ... and shifted. *What now?* They all took a quick step back—though not too far.

Bones, ligaments, organs, tissues, all of it crackled and morphed once more. In under a minute, Cassia was again a woman. A very naked woman, who looked just like Naya. The moment would have been far more awkward if nudity weren't a part of pack life.

"My body," Meiling said. "I want it back." She looked to the wizards, a determined draw to her mouth. "Is that possible?"

Mordecai waggled his mouth this way and that as he considered her question, but Albacus answered first: "If it's a matter of reversing the flow of energy, we should be able to do that, yes."

"Though we can't be certain what might happen to all the immortality magic you now house within you," Mordecai said. "Naya seems only to possess a small amount of it."

"You're saying if Meiling gets her body back," Naya said, "you might accidentally end up giving Cassia her immortality magic back?"

"It's a possibility worthy of consideration," Albacus said, twisting the end of one of his many braids in thought.

"Then we can't risk it," Maverick said in the commanding tone of his alpha wolf. "After all Naya and Meiling have done to bring about this result, we can't do anything that might give Cassia her power back."

Naya silently squeezed Meiling's hand. It was true. It was a risk they couldn't take. That didn't make it any easier for Meiling to swallow the fact that she'd be stuck in the body of the creepy immortal for the rest of her life.

"At least you're smoking hot now," Naya told her, forcing a laugh to cut the edge of Meiling's disappointment.

"I was 'smoking hot' before." Meiling frowned, her eyes heavy with regret. "And I liked myself."

Naya tried to imagine what it would be like to walk around in a foreign skin—worse, that of her captor, who'd masterminded every single part of her life as if she were nothing more significant than a throwaway puppet.

"Maybe we could try?" Naya asked Maverick. "There might be a way to ensure the immortality magic stays put. Albacus and Mordecai could find it. Or even that smart-sounding Sir Lancelot."

"I don't want the immortality magic either," Meiling said. "I don't want to live forever."

Neither did Naya. A nice, long life of centuries filled with Bruno sounded like just the right amount to her. Who'd want to outlive everyone they loved?

"One problem at a time," Maverick said. "I'm sorry, Meiling, but we have to kill Cassia. Now that she's mortal, she's gotta go. It's too dangerous to try to body swap you. Very little has gone down as we expected since this all started. She's been playing us all."

Maverick scowled so fiercely his canines dipped onto his lower lip, his eyes blazing with the gold of the pack's magic. "If we do anything that isn't certain, we might end right back up with an immortal we can't kill."

"That's right," Mordecai said. "Magic is as unpredictable as it is wonderful."

"Especially magic as powerful as this type," Albacus added.

"I understand," Meiling whispered, and Naya embraced her from the side. Her sister sounded as if her puppy just died.

Naya leaned her head on her shoulder. "Don't worry. Once the bitch is gone, we'll figure something out."

Meiling forced a tremulous smile. "Yeah. That sounds good."

Both women realized they were voicing hopes that might never come to fruition.

Bruno crouched next to Cassia's limp body, studying her face intently. "Before we kill her, should we not find out more about the other immortals? The Five, as you call them?"

Maverick and River smiled savagely. Maverick said, "Most definitely. We'll get every bit of information out of her while we can."

"No doubt about it," River said. "She'll talk."

Naya had never heard either her alpha or beta sound so vicious.

Immortals were their secret enemies, hiding in their midst as they did as they pleased, treating them like unimportant playthings. The wolves needed to find an advantage.

This battle might be over, but the war was far from won.

"The immortals run the hunters," Naya said to a chorus of furious grunts.

"Alpha," a woman's voice rang out from behind them. Naya turned to find Zasha and Quannah stepping out from the wolves gathered there. She hadn't realized they'd joined them.

"I'd like in on that interrogation," Zasha said.

The coming dawn, lightening the sky, illuminated the ferocity on the woman's face. With all of Maverick's and River's rippling muscles, Naya wasn't sure if they or Zasha would be the more brutal of the interrogators.

"I'd like to be there as well," added Quannah, Zasha's mate. His long face was stoic, unbreakable. "I have a few favors to pay back for how my woman was treated. I'd kill to get my hands on Cyrus."

Zasha smiled; retribution danced across her blue eyes. "*Lots* of favors to pay back." She slammed a fist into her open palm with a loud, crisp smack. Several wolves around her snarled in unison, getting on board with the plan.

Maverick announced, "The alpha and beta of the Smoky Mountain Pack are welcome to interrogate the prisoner." He glanced at Bruno. "The beta of the Andes Mountain Pack too, should he want to." A look at Boone, who stood back along with more shifters. "The beta of the Northwestern Pack as well. The Rocky Mountain Pack thanks you all for your support. You joined us in fighting a common enemy. You'll always have our loyalty, isn't that right, Rocky Mountain Pack?"

A chorus of assent rang out. Naya's heart began to feel lighter.

As much as the odds had been stacked against

them, they'd vanquished the great immortal. She was nothing more than a woman now, one who perhaps had a few tricks up her sleeves, but nothing they couldn't deal with, especially with the mages' help.

On cue, Maverick turned toward them: "My pack and I also owe you our gratitude and allegiance."

"Oh, we've had great fun," Albacus said, his voice as jovial as the chiming of the beads capping all that gray hair of his.

"Dear me, *oui*," Mordecai added. "The most fun we've had in ages."

It was official. The wizard brothers were as odd in their concept of fun as they were in everything else.

Bruno stood, leaving Cassia's side to drape an arm around Naya's shoulders. He pulled her close, but Naya didn't let go of Meiling. She had the feeling her sister needed her now more than ever.

River bent over to pick up Cassia, presumedly at the alpha's telepathic command to take her somewhere private for questioning, when Cassia's eyes popped open in her otherwise completely still body.

"Holy fuck," River said as he startled, then reached for her again.

Her eyes were the same crystalline blue as

Naya's—as Meiling's used to be and should have been.

Naya looked into them, figuring it'd be the very last time ... only to watch them change into a bright, luminescent violet.

The same color as immortality magic,

"Fuck," Naya muttered as she bent to retrieve Meiling's dao. The sentiment was repeated on all sides of her.

CHAPTER NINETEEN

NAYA

CASSIA WAS PUSHING to her feet.

Maverick and River tried to hold her down. Bruno, Scooby, Cleo, Zasha, and Quannah rushed over to help. A torrent of air pushed them, forcing the snarling shifters sliding back, ripping up grass and rocks as they went. Their muscles bulged and strained as they fought the invisible force, and other shifters ran over to assist.

Naya's pulse whooshed through her head so loudly that for a few instants it was all she could hear. Then Meiling asked, "What do we do?"

Meiling's chill-as-a-cucumber composure was shaky.

They'd already done everything they knew how to do!

"She doesn't have any immortality magic left. It

shouldn't be possible," Naya said as she cast a frantic look at the wizards. But they didn't answer the *What the hell do we do now?* question she silently broadcast their way. Their cheeks were ruddy despite their translucency as they flushed and scrambled to counteract Cassia's inexplicable control of the air. Already, their hoary beards and mustaches undulated as they bore down on the woman, chanting whatever spell they'd been using before to dampen her interference with the air currents.

"We have to kill her now," Naya told Meiling even as it became blatantly apparent that Cassia's ability to control the air was independent of her immortality. The woman still had magic of some sort, and that was a problem. A big, fat, bloody, serious-as-a-silver-blade-to-the-heart problem.

"How do we kill her?" Meiling asked as Naya withdrew her sword again. Naya's pistols were empty, but a big-ass silver blade should do the trick just fine if the bitch could die.

And she'd better.

Meiling drew a couple of the many blades strapped all around her body, but when the sisters moved toward Cassia, the force of a tornado slid them back.

Naya's eyes watered; her skin stung, the air pressing against her chest and stomach painfully.

She pushed on. So did Meiling.

The mages raised their voices until they were shouting above the whistling and whipping wind attempting to dash them all away.

Bruno, Maverick, and the rest were tilted at forty-five-degree angles, their feet digging divots into the wild grass.

Cassia, in the eye of the storm, threw her head back and opened her mouth, a chilling, haunting cackle rolling out. Her long blond hair, exactly like Naya's, didn't so much as billow. Not a single strand rose out of place.

Cassia laughed and laughed ... and then laughed some more, each time sending shivers down the length of Naya's body.

Move away from her, amor, Bruno said through his link to her. *Whatever is happening, Cassia seems more dangerous than before.*

No doubt, Naya responded, but had no intention of going anywhere. Cassia was hers to kill. She would escort her out of this world and straight to the gates of hell.

Cassia loosed an unhinged, maniacal giggle. Even the forest surrounding them seemed to recoil at its darkness. Then she stared straight at Naya, Meiling, and then back to Naya, her violet eyes burning brightly like pack magic. Only, it was nothing as pure or as balanced. It wasn't even like the immortality magic that simmered inside Naya, now a part of her.

This was something different. Something terrible.

"Do you feel that?" Naya whispered to Meiling, thinking Cassia wouldn't be able to hear them over the constant moaning of the wind.

"You mean the way her magic feels different now?" Meiling asked.

"Yep. It's not the same, right? It's not immortality magic anymore."

"I don't think it is, no."

"So do you think we can kill her?" Naya asked, clenching her hand around the hilt of her borrowed sword.

"I sure hope so."

"Well then, I'm itching to give it a go." But Naya hesitated. "Can you live with being stuck in her body?"

Meiling didn't answer right away, despite the urgency of their circumstances. But when she did, she sounded certain: "I can. I must. We can't do anything that might unleash whatever she is on the world. She feels..."

"Evil," Naya completed.

"Yes, dark, evil, disgusting."

"Little girls," Cassia said in a voice that was

deeper and more haunting than it'd been before. She spoke to them as if through a tunnel, her voice unmarred by the devastating currents around them.

"I am not evil. Darkness is not evil. It is merely *power*."

The word *power* echoed as if spoken through a megaphone.

Cassia continued. "I am more powerful than you could ever imagine. Your efforts to contain me are wasted. You cannot kill me."

"We took your immortality magic," Naya said, edging herself in front of her sister, attempting to draw the bulk of Cassia's focus.

With those eerie, glowing eyes, Cassia watched Naya for several moments, during which shifters all around them were struggling to reach Cassia—and failing.

"I know how to get it back," Cassia finally said, her voice ringing hollow, its pitch somehow off. "I've been stuck in Cassia's body for seven centuries. She didn't know, the stupid girl. But I've been watching her every move."

Naya felt her heart beat, her lungs inflate, the blood rushing through her body as everything around her stilled.

Say what?

She swallowed, and forced the question out,

making every effort not to sound as rattled as she was. "Who are you, then, if you're not Cassia?"

The responding smile, on appearance, seemed normal. Naya couldn't figure out what it was about the gesture, but it sent a chill racing through her as if she'd jumped into Arctic waters.

"I'm the original immortal, infant." Cassia's lip—so much like Naya's, which only made the scene that much more surreal—curled in abject disgust. "I am Cassia's father."

Meiling didn't visibly react beside Naya, but the werewolf in her could smell the spike in her sister's fear.

Apparently, so could Cassia's father. The woman with the glowing violet eyes smiled once more. Another dip in the Arctic bolted through Naya.

Cassia circled her head around her neck, a languorous movement, as if her efforts to keep the wind holding them all at bay were effortless.

"I would thank you for freeing me, but that might seem heartless of me since I'm still going to kill you. Every single one of you."

"Oh, and that's not fucking *heartless*, you bastard?" Naya spat out, barely able to handle the oddity of speaking to her lookalike, who was actually a man she'd never met.

Talk about *Fucked. Up.*

"Watch your tongue when you talk to your superiors, or I'll cut it out before I kill you."

Naya reeled back as if struck with a whip. There was power behind her—his—words. Magic of some sort.

"I am the original immortal. I am the first of my kind. You are but insignificant blips on the path of a dying comet."

"You can't kill us all," Meiling said.

"I can and I will." Another eerie smile, made all the creepier for the familiar features it crept across. "I'll need your life forces to power my own. It is your mortality that will again create the immortality my *daughter*"—he stopped to spit on the ground at his feet; the wind didn't touch the evidence of his hatred—"stole from me and then squandered. She was the brightest of them all, but not bright enough. Foolish, idiotic girl ... just like her sisters." He chuckled. "At least they served a purpose. They fueled a greater being. Their deaths had meaning."

Man, Naya was almost feeling sorry for Cassia. If she had this monster prick for a father, it might explain away some things...

"You killed Cassia's sisters?" Meiling asked.

"I accepted their sacrifices. Their worthwhile contributions."

"And did they willingly give their lives to you?" Meiling followed up.

"Of course not," he snapped. "They lacked my vision. But they were my daughters. My property. They were mine to do with as I pleased." He grimaced. "I favored Cassia, gave her the chance to be almost my equal. I gave her a gift I saved for her alone. And how did she thank me? By *betraying* me."

"Sounds to me like she did a plenty fine job of thanking you," Naya whipped. "You deserved what you got and then some."

"You ... dare?" he thundered, and a crack of power struck the earth beneath them as forcefully as lightning. The ground quaked. "You are an ant. An insect. A meaningless"—another lip curl—"woman."

"That motherfucker," Zasha yelled, echoing Naya's thoughts, and likely also Meiling's, but Naya didn't seek Zasha out.

The mages were shouting something in the background. Hoping it was some sort of plan, Naya wouldn't do anything to draw Creepy Asswad Father's attention to what was going on behind him.

"I'm bored of you," the asshole on a power trip said with a disinterested flick of his shoulders—her shoulders; still so weird.

He threw them back and began chanting in a deep and dangerous sounding Latin.

Behind him, Albacus and Mordecai shouted more frantically.

Keep him talking, Maverick said into her mind almost at the same time as Bruno said, *The wizards think they can cut off his control to the air element by linking to our life forces. Distract him.*

After only seconds of power-tripping dickwad's chanting, Naya could already feel power building in the crackling air around him. So she blurted out the first thing that came to mind. "If you're so powerful and almighty, how did your daughter get the upper hand over you?" She even inserted a taunting, mocking tone to her question to make sure she grabbed his attention.

He glared at her for so long and so hard that Naya had the distinct urge to look away.

She refused, cocking a hip out in defiance instead. "She *killed* you. She was obviously more powerful than you were. Stronger than you are now."

His nostrils flared and he roared, "I gave her immortality! I trusted her to understand the depth of gratitude she should have for me. She abused it."

"Yeah." Naya snorted in derision. "Sounds to me like you're the mack daddy of abusers. She duped you, plain and simple." Naya tilted her head in consideration. "And then you left her with a whole stinking heapload of daddy issues for the favor."

"You should know your place," he said in a single statement that reeked of peril. Naya's Sister Wolf was on alert inside her, ready to throw down with her.

"I do know my place. I am a representation of the divine feminine. I am grace and strength incarnate. I am the moon and the ocean tides. I am the balance of nature herself."

Naya had no idea where any of this was coming from, but it was enraging the hell out of Daddy Asshole, so she kept going.

"I am human and wolf. I am kindness and compassion, while I'm also punishment and retribution. I am motherfucking *woman* and you *will* hear me roar."

She threw her head back and let Sister Wolf's howl loose. All around her, howls erupted.

Her blood sister. Her pack sisters. Zasha.

And then also the men. Bruno first, then even Maverick and Quannah.

Fury colored Cassia's face in a red that became more vivid in the burgeoning dawn, but that wasn't what stole Naya's breath away.

Those violet eyes flickered blue.

Blue.

And behind Cassia, the wizards linked hands with the shifters. Their chanting rose in volume.

The whip and whistling of the air softened and ... dwindled.

Cassia's eyes flared violet again. "Daughter, know your place," he barked, no longer speaking to Naya, but to the daughter who remained alive and distinct inside the single body.

Hope sparked inside Naya.

"Of course I was alive inside you all this time. You didn't think you could actually end *me*, did you? If you did, you're even more foolish than I realized."

A pause during which Naya hoped Cassia was giving him hell.

"I waited and watched and listened. I always knew I'd have my chance to take over your body. I'll eventually have to switch over to the body of a man. But the weaker sex will serve me for the time being. And this body is strong for a woman."

Naya and Meiling both growled.

Naya was going to skin the dick alive rather than let him walk around in their body.

He laughed. "I should have killed you along with your sisters. That was my only mistake. You looked like me, and so I assumed you'd be like me. I won't err in that way ever again. Time for you to die like your sisters." The smile grew colder. "They screamed when their end arrived. Weak, frightened babes. A waste of my seed."

Cassia's eyes widened in shock and then her mouth dropped open in evident surprise. Next, a roar as ferocious as a male lion's tore out of Cassia's mouth. It rang on, and Naya's Sister Wolf responded, ready to rally and join the fight.

Cassia's eyes flashed with the brightness of the sun—and then her eyes shone blue.

With those crystalline blue eyes, Cassia bore down on Naya.

"Throw me your blade."

"What? Fuck no," Naya said automatically.

Cassia tsked, then positioned her right hand over her breast, above her heart, and began digging into her flesh.

Blood pooled and ran down her nude stomach. Cassia only renewed her efforts, scooping out her skin. Her mouth twisted in concentration.

"Damn, that's..." Naya lacked the words. That was determined. Cassia was trying to scoop out her own heart.

To kill her father, Naya realized with a stark rush of truth.

Without pausing to debate the move, Naya whistled.

Cassia looked up. Naya grabbed Meiling's sword by its tip and tossed it across the body length that separated them.

The wind died completely, and Cassia caught the sword adeptly by the hilt.

Without so much as pausing, she carved a hole around her heart and tossed the blade to the side. She reached a hand inside the now-gaping cavity and yanked the bloody, still-beating heart out, ripping it free of the surrounding arteries.

"No, Father," Cassia said in a fading voice. "*You* are the one who must die."

She crumpled to the ground in an inglorious heap. "For my sisters," she whispered.

She blinked heavily, the glow in her blue eyes fading.

CHAPTER TWENTY

CASSIA

SHE HAD ONLY MOMENTS LEFT. Without a heart, this body wouldn't continue for long. It was only the trace remnants of immortality magic allowing her consciousness to linger at all.

If not that, it was the obstinate will of the brutish and severe man who was her father. He expected everyone and everything in existence to obey his will. Demanded it even, the consummate prick. He was like a parasite who adapted and endured. He'd studied and learned the dark magical arts. He'd likely traded his soul for the spell that would allow him to live forever. She should have known that a man as unkillable as he would be one and the same as his magic, his power an evil that would infect her when she invited it into her heart.

She could scarcely believe her father had

remained alive within her for centuries. But even less could she comprehend that she hadn't noticed how he was changing her. She'd once been as kind and compassionate as her six sisters. She'd never allowed anyone, besides her father, to walk all over her, but neither had she been cruel, even when she had to stand up for herself. The woman she'd been so long ago would never have done the things she had. She'd imprisoned Édouard and hundreds of vampires in lives of servitude, worse even than the one her father had subjected her to when he'd feigned to be a family man. Never would she have earned the moniker of Kiss of Death.

That wasn't her.

That was *him*.

She'd believed herself a powerful being cursed to an eternal life when really she'd been a meat suit lacking in her own guidance. He'd simply jumped vessels to command her ship. It had been foolish of her, really, not to foresee that enough of his personality would be wrapped up in his immortality magic that when she pulled it into herself, she'd be absorbing his essence as well. She'd killed only his body, nothing else. During the long reign of her ignorance, he'd grown stronger and imposed his orders on her more easily.

At least before he'd made her immortal she'd

rebelled against his decisions, if only on the inside. What he'd done to her since was worse. More masterful. She was the oblivious puppet who thought she was a real woman. It was the worst of violations.

Where she was going, however, she didn't guess there was room for regret. Her entire life had been her father's. But he wouldn't have her death.

When she went, she'd rid the world of him. It wouldn't make up for the injury she'd caused over the centuries, but it was a start, an important one.

She could feel him inside, resisting, fighting to hang on. But now that she was dying, he was weaker than ever before. He had nothing to hang on to.

His essence was the first to go. She didn't bother saying a farewell or a hearty *fuck you forever, Father dearest,* focusing instead on the sudden lightness that filled what remained of her being.

He drifted away, and when he was gone it was as if she could breathe fully for the first time since she'd learned of her sisters' deaths. She assumed it was a metaphoric feeling, since she couldn't sense any of her body's functions anymore.

Even so, those final moments were the best she'd experienced in a thousand years. She blinked and watched as the sun burst above mountain peaks painted with trees in a blast of light that suggested all the color that was soon to surge across the vast sky.

The dawn brought hope, peace, and liberty—freedom from her father's tyranny. When she was truly alive, still human, it's what she and her sisters had yearned for, and once he'd killed them and foisted the immortality spell on her, she'd longed to rid herself of the weight of his actions.

She closed her eyes. No sounds reached her; it was all hazy anyway. No longer could she sense the air along her bare skin, or the blood that coated her abdomen and legs, or the stares of the many supernaturals surrounding her, who'd bear witness to her final death.

The sun warmed her face as the childlike giggles of her sisters rang through her. She smiled, or at least she thought she did. Though they laughed together, she could distinguish the unique tonality of each of her sisters. Her best friends. Her only true companions in life.

Their joy was more like magic than anything Cassia had encountered in the rare, arcane, esoteric library she'd collected. The sound of their joy was more enchanting than any spell, shapeshifter, or sorcery. It grew louder, nearer, until Cassia could make out the faces of one sister after the next, all hovering over her, smiling ... waiting.

The years and then the centuries had dulled her memory of her sisters' faces, despite her fervent efforts to hold on to every piece of them she could. Now, she could make out every detail, every unique curve of their brows and lips, the exact angle of their chins and cheekbones, the way their eyes sparkled, their cheeks flushed pink, and their grins widened as, one by one, each of them extended a hand to her, the part of their set who had been absent for so long, the missing piece to the whole—the broken link that would bond them all together.

As Cassia reached for her sisters, she released every one of her burdens, casting them away without so much as a thought.

True freedom was finally hers. Once elusive, it filled her.

She was as light and bright as the rising sun.

EPILOGUE
BRUNO

AS HE USUALLY DID, Bruno woke before Naya, fluttering his eyes open to groggily assure himself she was exactly where she belonged—in his arms—before closing them again and pulling her closer. It was shortly after dawn, and the light was just beginning to filter in through the cracks in the drapes.

They'd shared her cabin—and her bed—for the last four months. Her scent, her body, her smile, all had become as familiar to him as his own. Never had Brother Wolf felt more settled. Never more content.

Naya was his mate. She was his woman.

And every part of him, body and soul, was hers, through and through.

After the death of the immortal Cassia, Maverick had joined forces with the Smoky Mountain Pack to search for any signs of the remaining immortals, especially Cyrus. But not only had none of the many shifters found sign of them, but the hunters had been quiet as well. The hunters were never quiet for long, and yet there'd been no attacks at all on any of the packs in the Americas, not through an entire season. It had everyone both equally relieved and on edge. Bruno, like many others, like Naya, was uneasy trusting that the constant persecution and hunting of wolf shifters should end so easily. He suspected it was more of a respite. A temporary reprieve.

Even so, he'd take it.

Once Maverick had decided his wolves were under no immediate threat, he'd finally relented and given Naya and Bruno his blessing on their union. Maverick had surprised Bruno by being the one to suggest a mate ceremony. Not even the alpha could deny that Bruno and Naya were mates. Their love for each other was so strong, Bruno imagined that beings as aware as wolf shifters couldn't help but sense their connection.

It was undeniable. Inevitable. Eternal.

The ceremony had been as simple as it had been beautiful. Naya had dressed in an unadorned gossamer gown and Clove had crowned her head in the vibrant blooms of summer. Fresh-faced and bare-foot, Naya had never looked more stunning as when she linked hands with him and spoke her vows to love and cherish him—and his wolf—for the rest of their long lives.

Bruno's heart had swelled, making speech difficult. He'd spied Maverick discreetly dabbing his eyes and wiping his nose, though no one dared insinuate that the alpha was overcome by emotion, while officiating as the infant he'd so long ago been entrusted with set the course of her life as a woman.

A strong, incredible, fine woman. Bruno draped a leg over her bare thighs and tightened his arm around her torso. Even after waking with her every morning since her escape from Cassia, he still was stunned by his good fortune.

She murmured and smiled, that private smile she gave only him, and wriggled her hips closer to his.

Softly, he inhaled the scents of her hair and skin, and Brother Wolf grumbled happily inside. He'd been a big, mushy, floofball lately, though Bruno didn't let on that he noticed. Brother Wolf was a prideful creature.

Absently, Bruno trailed his fingertips across Naya's shoulder. Her skin was soft and supple. He'd memorized every inch, and loved the scars as much as the unmarred stretches.

"Mmmmmm, hey there, handsome," Naya said, her voice soft, husky, and sensual. Her long lashes continued to rest against her cheeks.

"*Buen día, peligrosa.*" He kissed her closest shoulder, then slid his lips down her arm.

Her eyelids fluttered open and her smile grew. "Hmm-mmm. Keep going."

As usual, Bruno was only too happy to do as she asked. He thought he'd never tire of indulging her. Her every wish was his command, though he wouldn't be telling his fiery love that anytime soon. He might not be as prideful as his wolf, but he was well aware he'd been mooning over the woman. He couldn't help himself, not even when Jeb and Howie wouldn't stop telling him how *whipped* he was. He figured both men would only understand if they ever found their own mates.

Bruno ran his fingers gingerly over the long scar that tapered across her abdomen, a ready reminder of just how lucky he was to be able to share his life with her.

"Today's the day," he whispered into her hair. "Are you ready?"

"To start my new life with you?"

"*Sí.*" He dragged kisses along her collarbone.

She giggled when his kiss became barely a whisper and it tickled. "Of course I am." Her eyes opened and met his. "You think I'm gonna like it there?"

Bruno pushed to his elbow and smiled down at

her. Distracted by all the danger and excitement, he hadn't realized just how much he'd missed his Andes Mountains until he'd contemplated returning.

Maverick was reluctant to see Naya go, but he said he understood, after eliciting a promise from her that she wouldn't stay away forever. That she'd return to visit. Across a thick throat, he'd even uttered the phrase, "Come back to your father." He'd never referred to himself as Naya's father before, but the title was apt, and Naya had readily fallen into his embrace.

Bruno studied the woman who looked so much like his alpha, and so much like the cursed immortal immediately before her death. But the resemblance was only on the physical level. Bruno saw a deeper part of her, where her love for nature resided, where her wolf and connectedness to the energy that circulated through all of life thrived.

"Sí, peligrosa, I think you're going to love it there. But we don't have to stay for long if you don't want to."

She turned to face him. "But will Lara be okay when you want to leave with me?" It was a common question in their discussions of late. But never was it *if* Bruno wanted to depart with her. They both understood there was no separating them now.

"She'll understand," Bruno said. "She's an alpha,

and a very intuitive and wise one. She understands what it's like to be a mate, even if she hasn't yet found hers."

"But you're her beta."

"I am. And it's the pack magic that's selected me for the role. However, if in time we decide it's not right for us anymore, there will always be another shifter who can take my place as beta." He paused to stare deep into her eyes so she could feel the veracity of his intentions. "I don't need to lead others. What I do need is to be at your side and to feel you happy. Whatever we decide from here on out, we decide together."

She nodded, but her mouth twisted left then right; she was deep in thought. Then, "You think Lara's gonna flip when she sees me?"

He chuckled. "I'm quite certain she will be shocked, there's no doubt about it."

He'd corresponded with his alpha via mail. It had been his only option. And though he'd revealed the existence of his mate, and thus received Lara's permission to extend his leave, he hadn't told her exactly *who* his mate was.

There were some surprises in life that were worth waiting for.

"I can hardly wait to see what she'll say," Bruno added. Again, he chuckled. Not only was Lara his alpha, but she was also his friend. His arrival with her identical sister was just the kind of event he imagined could at last unsettle his constantly even-keeled alpha, and that would be fun to experience.

Naya's next question was softer, more vulnerable. "Do you think she'll like me?"

He snorted. "Why wouldn't she? As Clove likes to say, you kick ass, take names, and then do it all over again."

Naya laughed, and the sound lightened his already buoyant heart.

But then she said, "I'm gonna miss that fucker. There's no one else like her."

"Is that a bad thing though?"

She barked out another laugh. "I don't think the world could handle another her. But she's still my girl, and I'm gonna miss the fuck out of her."

"She and her new man can visit whenever they want."

She smiled. "Yeah. I'm gonna make her visit." But clouds had come out to conceal the sunny skies in her bright blue eyes.

Bruno had extended the same invitation to Meiling, who'd already departed. Though Albacus and Mordecai had successfully separated the sisters' merged life-force energies, Naya had mourned Meiling's absence as if the two of them had been raised together. Bruno suspected Meiling would be feeling their separation as acutely, and that she'd make an appearance on his pack lands before too long.

Once she discovered Li Kāng's fate.

"Tell me what it's like there," Naya asked of him, and not for the first time.

"Well," he began, running his hand up and down her bare waist, across her hip, down the side of her thigh. "It's somewhat like here, only—"

"You know what? Never mind. I don't want to talk anymore."

"Oh." His eyebrows arched in mock consternation. As if he didn't know what she wanted by now. He could smell her arousal, a heavenly fragrance in the air. It was the most intoxicating scent he'd ever smelled. It filled his nostrils and garbled his thoughts. "Tell me," he said, voice low and deep with his own need.

"Ah-uh." She dragged her lips across her lower lip. His dick finished hardening at her devil-may-care look; he knew all too well what it led to.

She looped her top arm over his back, then slid it down and across his tight abdomen, around his thighs, where she gripped his ass and squeezed—hard. Then, with mischief sparking in her eyes, she slid her fingers back along his thigh, leaving torturous tingles in her wake, drew them too fucking slowly back toward his center...

She wrapped her fingers around his cock and grinned, waggling her brows. "*This*. This is what I want. Right. The fuck. Now."

She opened her mouth to say something else, but he crushed his lips against hers before she could, and in an instant was gasping and panting and long past thought.

She draped her leg across his hips, pulling him tightly against her. He lined up with her center and slid inside her.

It didn't matter that later that day they'd begin traveling toward the Andes and his pack.

He was already home.

———

Naya

Three hours later, a grinning Bruno left to ready his motorcycle for their departure. Naya was packing up her final things. Though she didn't have many personal effects, never needing all that much, she wanted to take as much of home with her as she could.

Maverick had gifted her another wolf pendant to

replace the one Meiling had lost. This one was tracker free, and made from solid gold. Naya pressed a hand against it as she often did, loving the feel of home that she was taking with her. The Rocky Mountain Pack would always be her family, no matter where she and Bruno ended up living, and the Rockies would always be a part of her, as innate as her fingerprints. She had a feeling she'd dream of these peaks, even when she was surrounded by others in the Andes.

With all the clothes she wanted to take fitting into a single duffel bag, she added her favorite climbing shoes on top. She could get harnesses, carabiners, and rope anywhere, but her favorite shoes were worn in to perfection. Naya was entertaining the idea of climbing professionally for a while. Now that she was no longer anyone's savior and didn't have to hide, she could compete alongside the greatest climbers in the world, including many members of her own pack, like Howie and Jeb.

First, she and Bruno would spend a little time with his pack—she swallowed instinctively—with the sister who didn't even know she existed. But after, they might travel the world, climbing, exploring, adventuring, seeing all the sights she'd dreamed of and believed forever out of her reach.

Perhaps they'd travel to China again and visit

Meiling while Naya put to rest some of her demons—AKA memories of her time with Cassia and the brutal vampires.

Even though Meiling had left only a month before, staying in their Moonlit Mountains longer than Naya could have hoped, she already missed her. And it wasn't because their life forces were magically bonded anymore; the wizards had successfully separated them. Even so, Naya couldn't be certain if the bond she felt to Meiling was simply that of a sister, since she'd never had one before, or if the time they'd been linked had connected them in an extraordinary way.

Before the wizards left, they'd overseen Naya giving the bit of immortality magic she'd possessed to Meiling. Naya had wanted to keep it—not because she desired it, but because she didn't want Meiling alone to shoulder the burden of a magic that might still contain some of Cassia. But it had been that very reason that Meiling used to convince her to give it all to Meiling. Better for only one of them to have to deal with it than both of them, she'd said, especially when Meiling was off to hopefully find Li Kāng miraculously alive, and if not, to avenge his murder, and then confront the master vampires about how they'd hidden her true nature from her all her life—how they'd done Cassia's bidding instead of protected her; how they'd taken her on as an acolyte to a martial art that claimed to teach a balance of chi and power through mastering one's nature. The masters were frauds, she'd insisted. No one could achieve true mastery without integrity.

They weren't deserving guardians of the sacred book at the heart of Seimei Do.

She figured immortality would come in handy when facing off against a bunch of undead power-houses who didn't die easily. On that front, Naya couldn't argue, and if having all of the immortality magic could support Meiling, she was relieved to be free of it.

Meiling hadn't shared what exactly she was plan-ning. Naya suspected her sister was still figuring things out, but so far the larger supernatural world, including the vampires, was unaware Cassia was dead—and Meiling looked exactly like her.

In exchange, Meiling had left her a little parting gift. After Meiling had pulled Naya's immortality out through her breath, she'd shared her shifter magic.

Whatever Cassia's scientists had injected Meiling with, it had successfully altered her makeup. Meiling was no longer beholden to the cycles of the moon—and now neither was Naya. The two sisters could shift at will and without pain.

Naya had never loved her sister—or her wolf —more.

She was beginning a new stage of her life, one totally free of all limitations and constraints. And with her ferociously hot mate at her side to boot.

Life was looking, not just good, but amazing.

Naya slid Meiling's sheathed sword between her clothes. It had been another gift, one Naya readily accepted. With its intricate etchings, now scrubbed free of Cassia's blood, the blade was beautiful. But beyond that, it was her sister's. For that reason alone, Naya would treasure it.

Turning, she grabbed her second favorite blades from atop her nightstand and began wrapping them for packing. They were her second favorites because she'd given Meiling, aficionado of all things lethal, sharp, and shiny, her preferred set of blades. Meiling had hugged them to her chest like a treasure, gratitude beaming through her violet eyes.

Naya couldn't help but smile at the memory of the deadly martial artist Meiling squealing like a little kid at her gift.

Her sister was off on her own adventure, a much more dangerous one than Naya's.

But despite the relative quiet in the wolf shifter community over the past months, several of them were heading back into danger. Albacus and

Mordecai had returned to their academies, citing urgency with another enemy they referred to as the Voice, a group of assholes imbued with supernatural powers who kept attempting power grabs. Of course, the mages had used different language, and had been far less succinct in their expression of the problem they currently faced, but the gist of that matter was that there were creeps all around the world who wanted what wasn't theirs, and were willing to hurt others to get it.

Maverick, Zasha, and Quannah had offered their packs' assistance. Boone was apparently already involved, traveling with the wizards. If the Rocky Mountain Pack joined this fight, Naya might return to help.

And that might not be the only reason for her return. Even though Cassia was truly dead, and they'd burned her body until nothing was left but ashes, there were other immortals out there.

There was a man named Gideon in the Smoky Mountain Pack who'd once been a hunter, until he'd figured out he was on the wrong side of the fight. Since then, he'd chosen to become a werewolf, and he'd been one of the lucky ones strong enough to survive the first shift. From how Quannah told the story, the bastard was too stubborn to die, and was now part of their fold.

Gideon had steadily been working to infiltrate the Protectors of Humanity, as the hunters called themselves—ludicrous. Though he hadn't turned many hunters over to his new point of view, he had learned enough to discover that Cassia wasn't part of the infamous Five.

Which meant that there were at least five more immortals out there; one of them was Cyrus. Not only was he an immortal *and* some sort of dark mage, a terrifying combination, but he was apparently the mastermind behind the Pound, underground fighting rings that pitted wolf against wolf, and the man didn't much care whether his fighters were born wolves or if had to force the change on them.

Zasha, Quannah, and Gideon had been searching for the Five, and Cyrus especially, without luck. No new locations of the Pound had popped up —at least none that they'd heard of.

And every single wolf shifter out there was paying attention, looking for anything out of place, any sign that the immortals and their puppets, the hunters, were launching an attack.

After so many centuries of shifters having to constantly glance over their shoulders and sleep with one proverbial eye open, the peace felt unnatural, their safety elusive and uncertain. They continued to train as hard as ever, to build up their defenses, and to invent ways to counteract the hunters' pervasive use of silver infused weaponry.

When the immortals and hunters finally popped back up on the radar, the wolf shifters would be ready. At least, they'd be as ready as they could be.

The life of a shifter was never free of dangers, but Naya wouldn't trade her Sister Wolf for anything in the world. With her wolf, Naya felt more alive than any human. She experienced life both through her intellect and through raw power. As a very part of nature, experiencing her ebbs and flows. Feeling her strength. Her magic.

Yes, Naya's life would never be safe, but the sunshine tingled across her skin, the air vibrated and hummed, and the full force of life pumped through her veins.

She felt fully and riotously alive. Every moment was filled with magic and sensation.

Death came for everyone eventually, even immortals, especially now that they knew how to kill them. Meiling, with her own immortality, was a guarded secret. When the shifters found the others, they'd call on her.

But though death was inevitable, few lived in constant awe of the true gift that was life. And Naya was awe*struck*. In a short time, everything about her existence had been radically transformed.

Scanning her cabin, Naya didn't spot anything left to pack. She stuffed her toothbrush in a side pocket of her luggage and zipped up the bag with a sense of finality that left her tingling in anticipation.

When she opened her front door for the final time, bag in hand, she found Clove standing in front of it, fist poised to knock.

Clove's eyes widened as they landed on Naya's duffel. "You're ... ready to go? So soon?"

So soon? The couple of months Bruno had planned to stay had turned into four because Naya and Clove hadn't been ready to part.

Naya opened her mouth for a snappy retort, but nothing came out when she took in her fiery friend. The spark that usually illuminated Clove's eyes with an overdose of snarky spunk was absent. Even her pixie cut fell flat, droopy around her face.

"Oh fuck," Naya said instead, dropping her bag and yanking Clove into a crushing hug. "I'm gonna miss you too much."

Clove tucked her head into Naya's shoulder and sniffled. "You're an asshole for leaving me."

"Aww, you won't even miss me with all the fine shifter dick you'll be getting."

Clove chuckled, her laugh thick. "You're right. I won't even remember your name in another month with Lucian."

Huffing in mock offense, Naya pushed Clove out of her arms. Her friend laughed, and clung on in a side embrace.

While Quannah had been alpha of the Smoky Mountain Pack, Lucian had been his right-hand man. Now that Zasha and Quannah led their pack together, Lucian had come out to assist in the search for the immortals. When he'd laid eyes on Clove, sparks had flown, and the two had been attached at the hip—more like, the *loins*—ever since.

"You're probably gonna be heading out to the Smokies soon anyway," Naya said.

Clove grinned sheepishly before allowing her expression to morph into her usual devilry. "I will follow that man, and his fancy equipment, to the ends of the earth. Just don't tell him that. I don't want him to get cocky."

Naya chuckled. "I'm pretty sure he already knows you're smitten with him."

Clove slapped her on the bicep. "You take that back. I don't do all that sickly sweet mushy crap that you and Bruno do. I am *not* smitten."

Another chuckle. "You sure as shit are." Clove opened her mouth. "But don't worry, that man can't take his eyes off you. If you've got a dose of the *smittens*, he's got a double dose of it."

Clove cocked out a hip, pouting seductively. "How's a man supposed to resist all this anyway?"

Naya barked a laugh. "True. Lucian doesn't stand a chance. Life with you is gonna be a fucking trip, no doubt about it."

Hands on her hips, Clove nodded seriously. "You'd better believe it. I'm never gonna let him forget how good he's got it."

Draping an arm around her shorter friend's shoulders, Naya said, "I think he already knows it." She picked up her bag with the other hand. "Come on. Walk with me."

Clove stilled, making Naya pause in mid-step. "Is it already time to leave? Like, *now* now?"

"Yep, *now* now. I already said bye to Mav and everybody else before they headed out to follow up on a lead."

Clove resumed walking. "The Pound?"

"Something like that. A rumor that a fighting ring popped up somewhere, but Mav wasn't sure the lead would pan out. Might just be a dog fighting ring."

"Even so..."

"Even so, they'll shut that shit down. There's nothing worse than pit fighting."

"Fuck those assholes," Clove growled. "I'll throw *them* into a fighting pit, see how they like that messed-up shit."

"If only we could," Naya said. "That'd be easy. Throw all the immortals and hunters in a pit together."

"Let them wipe each other out. They can feel all good inside for making the world a better place as they die a painful death."

"That's right." Naya leaned her head on Clove's as they walked. "I'm gonna miss you so much."

Clove sniffled. "Damn fucking allergies." Allergies that wolf shifters didn't suffer from...

After a few more *allergy* sniffles, Clove said, "You know Mav just made up a bullshit excuse to get out of here, right?"

"Whaddya mean?"

"He's been an emotional basket case all week, knowing you're leaving. Snarling at everyone. He just couldn't handle seeing you ride off."

Naya sighed sadly. She was going to miss him. Everyone...

"Don't go getting all sad on me," Clove said. "You're gonna make me get all blotchy, and you know how awesome my complexion is." She squeezed Naya's side. "We'll see each other soon. Either you'll visit me, I'll drag that fine man of mine halfway across the world to visit you, or we'll meet up somewhere. Maybe Paris or Rome or ... oooh, a beach somewhere, with white sand and turquoise water. We can all skinny dip."

Naya smiled. "That sounds really nice, Clove. That's a plan."

"And a promise."

"And a promise," Naya repeated.

"Pinky swear?" Clove extended her little finger.

"All day long." Naya hooked her pinky through Clove's.

They walked like that all the way to Bruno's Harley-Davidson SuperLow, where the man already stood, waiting for Naya.

When he saw her, his green-blue-brown eyes lit up, and his smile was as bright as the morning sunshine. He took her bag from her and busied himself strapping it onto the back of his bike, which they'd leave at the airport for a pack member to retrieve for them. They'd be back for it.

Naya squeezed her friend as tightly as she could, so the feeling would last, then kissed the top of her crown. For the first time in their entire long friendship, Clove didn't complain.

"I love you, Clove," Naya whispered into her hair.

"I love you too, boo," Clove said, tears flowing openly down her cheeks.

"You be good," Naya said over her own tears.

"And by that I mean, have fun being your badass self."

"You too, girl. You too."

Then, before the two women could break down, Naya hopped on the back of the motorcycle behind Bruno, wrapped her arms around him, and blew Clove wet, and possibly snotty, kisses.

Let's go, Naya told Bruno through their link. *Time to start our new adventure together.*

He kickstarted the bike, and as it rumbled beneath her thighs, he said, *Te amo, peligrosa. I'm so very grateful to be on this journey with you.*

Overwhelmed by his sentiment and Clove's glistening puppy-dog eyes, all she could do was nod against his back and wave at her best friend.

And as they roared down the road, toward the exit of pack lands, after which they'd take a circuitous route in case any hunters might be watching despite their silence, Naya focused only on the feel of the man in her arms, the wind whipping through her hair, and the lightness in her heart.

She'd never imagined it would happen, but now she was truly free of her prison.

The day, the world, and her future were so very bright.

She was coming for them...

AMID AN ENDING, A BEGINNING

UP on the bluffs of the Scottish Highlands, deep in a dense forest populated by ancient trees, a wolf shifter pup scents life deep beneath the earth.

He digs insistently at the grave, whining, and when no one comes, he howls, drawing the attention of his pack.

Beneath the dark, cold dirt, within her tomb, a being—dormant, not dead—stirs.

Then, she awakens...

AFTERWORD

Naya and Bruno's story has come to an end, but that doesn't mean the adventure is over! There is so much more I intend to explore in this rich, vibrant, and incredibly dangerous world.

Follow Meiling in *Return of the Viper* as she returns to Shèng Shān Monastery to hold the vampire masters accountable for their sins. She's going to put all those years of martial arts training, along with that sliver of immortality magic, to kickass use, in fine Seimei Do style.

And also read Davina's story in *Immortal Howl* as she proves that there are some wills strong enough to survive even death. You didn't think one of Naya's sisters was going to go down and stay down, did you? ;)

The new series, *Warrior Monks* and *Highlands*

Pack, are the direct continuations of both the *Rocky Mountain Pack* and the previous *Smoky Mountain Pack* series.

Cassia might be dead, along with her despicable father, but they weren't the only immortals prowling the earth. And those vampire masters ... nasty business. It's time for these warrior women to take up the fight where Naya left off.

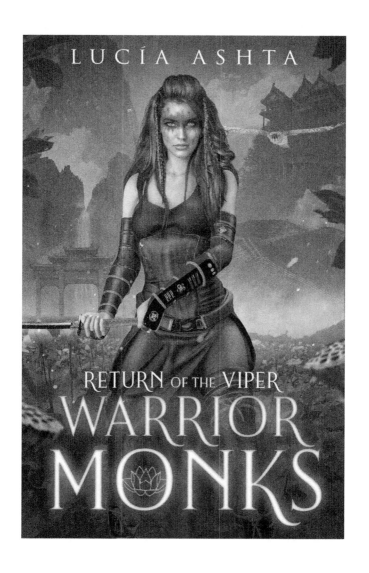

Warrior Monks

Book One

Return of the Viper

Continue the adventures with Meiling in *Return of the Viper*, coming soon!

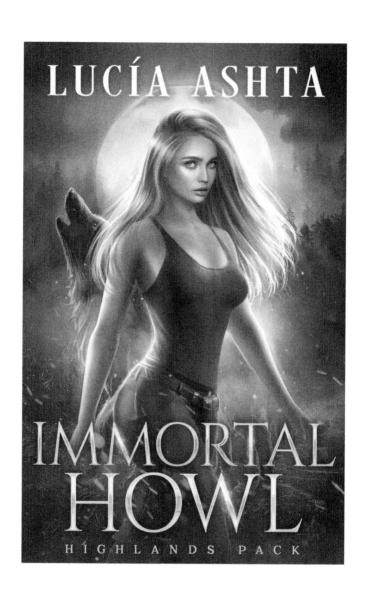

Highlands Pack
Book One
Immortal Howl

And continue the adventures with Davina in *Immortal Howl*, also coming soon!

BOOKS BY LUCÍA ASHTA

~ FANTASY & PARANORMAL BOOKS ~

WITCHING WORLD UNIVERSE

Warrior Monks
Return of the Viper
(coming soon)

Highlands Pack
Immortal Howl
(coming soon)

Magical Enforcers
Voice of Treason
(coming soon)

Magical Dragons Academy

Fae Rider

(coming soon)

Six Shooter and a Shifter

When the Moon Shines

When the Sun Burns

When the Lightning Strikes

When the Dust Settles

Rocky Mountain Pack

Wolf Bonds

Wolf Lies

Wolf Honor

Wolf Destinies

Smoky Mountain Pack

Forged Wolf

Beta Wolf

Blood Wolf

Witches of Gales Haven

Perfect Pending

Magical Mayhem

Charmed Caper

Smexy Shenanigans

Homecoming Hijinks
Pesky Potions

Magical Creatures Academy

Night Shifter
Lion Shifter
Mage Shifter
Power Streak
Power Pendant
Power Shifter
Power Strike

Sirangel

Siren Magic
Angel Magic
Fusion Magic

Magical Arts Academy

First Spell
Winged Pursuit
Unexpected Agents
Improbable Ally
Questionable Rescue
Sorcerers' Web
Ghostly Return
Transformations

Castle's Curse
Spirited Escape
Dragon's Fury
Magic Ignites
Powers Unleashed

Witching World

Magic Awakens
The Five-Petal Knot
The Merqueen
The Ginger Cat
The Scarlet Dragon
Spirit of the Spell
Mermagic

Light Warriors

Beyond Sedona
Beyond Prophecy
Beyond Amber
Beyond Arnaka

PLANET ORIGINS UNIVERSE

Dragon Force

Invisible Born
Invisible Bound
Invisible Rider

Planet Origins

Planet Origins
Original Elements
Holographic Princess
Purple Worlds
Mowab Rider
Planet Sand
Holographic Convergence

OTHER WORLDS

Supernatural Bounty Hunter

(co-authored with Leia Stone)
Magic Bite
Magic Sight
Magic Touch

STANDALONES

Huntress of the Unseen
A Betrayal of Time
Whispers of Pachamama
Daughter of the Wind
The Unkillable Killer
Immortalium

~ ROMANCE BOOKS ~

ACKNOWLEDGMENTS

I'd write no matter what, because telling stories is a passion, but the following people make creating worlds (and life) a joy. I'm eternally grateful for the support of my beloved, James, my mother, Elsa, and my three daughters, Catia, Sonia, and Nadia. They've always believed in me, even before I published a single word. They help me see the magic in the world around me, and more importantly, within.

I'm thankful for every single one of you who've reached out to tell me that one of my stories touched you in one way or another, made you laugh or cry, or kept you up long past your bedtime. You've given me additional reason to keep writing.

My thanks also go to my beta reader team, advance reader team, and reader group. Your constant enthusiasm for my books makes every moment spent on my stories all that much more rewarding. I am grateful for your support.

ABOUT THE AUTHOR

Lucía Ashta is the Amazon top 20 bestselling author of young adult, new adult, and adult fantasy and paranormal fiction, including the series *Smoky Mountain Pack, Witches of Gales Haven, Magical Creatures Academy, Witching World, Dragon Force,* and *Supernatural Bounty Hunter.*

She is also the author of contemporary romance books.

When Lucía isn't writing, she's reading, painting, or adventuring. Magical fantasy is her favorite, but the romance and quirky characters are what keep her hooked on books.

A former attorney and architect, she's an Argentinian-American author who lives in North Carolina's Smoky Mountains with her family. She published her first story (about an unusual Cockatoo) at the age of eight, and she's been at it ever since.

Sign up for Lucía's newsletter:
https://www.subscribepage.com/LuciaAshta

Hang out with her:
https://www.facebook.com/groups/LuciaAshta

Connect with her online:
LuciaAshta.com
AuthorLuciaAshta@gmail.com

facebook.com/authorluciaashta

bookbub.com/authors/lucia-ashta

amazon.com/author/luciaashta

instagram.com/luciaashta

Printed in Great Britain
by Amazon

10916856R00185